# THE JURY ON SMOKY HILL

# THE JURY ON SMOKY HILL

## JACK CURTIS

THORNDIKE
CHIVERS

This Large Print book is published by Thorndike Press®, Waterville, Maine USA and by BBC Audiobooks, Ltd, Bath, England.

Published in 2004 in the U.S. by arrangement with Golden West Literary Agency.

Published in 2004 in the U.K. by arrangement with Golden West Literary Agency.

U.S.  Hardcover 0-7862-6460-8  (Western)
U.K.  Hardcover 0-7540-6954-0  (Chivers Large Print)
U.K.  Softcover  0-7540-6955-9  (Camden Large Print)

The text of this Large Print edition is unabridged.
Other aspects of the book may vary from the original edition.

Set in 16 pt. Plantin by Ramona Watson.

Printed in the United States on permanent paper.

**British Library Cataloguing-in-Publication Data available**

**ISBN 0-7862-6460-8 (lg. print : hc : alk. paper)**

# THE JURY ON SMOKY HILL

# 1

From the *Ellsworth Record Republican Weekly*: *"Ellsworth, Kansas, May 15, 1873. Big Ben Thompson, an able and truculent gunfighter, was disarmed yesterday by Wyatt Earp in front of a hundred cowboy friends. His gun was confiscated by Marshal Hogue who returned it to Thompson this morning when the Texas gambler had sobered up. . . ."*

Within a month Earp, Thompson, and Hogue went their separate ways, Earp to Wichita, Thompson to Abilene, Hogue "west."

Marshal Hogue's departure created a vacancy which had to be filled quickly because the great cattle herds were arriving, with their untamed drovers ready to tree the town.

The city council selected a young rancher named Dave Cromwell, a six-footer with bulldogger shoulders and an honest face.

Dave Cromwell was picked because first of all, he was from Coleman County,

Texas, and therefore should understand the Texas cowboys' rampaging through town. Second, he was big and strong, with level, honest eyes, and though generally peaceable, he had never been known to back up from or lose a fight. Third, he'd bought an abandoned ranch over towards Lincoln on Bullfoot Creek and therefore was not just another transient gunfighter looking to skim off the cream and keep on going. Fourth, he needed the money.

Deputy Lou Wolford, a whole and entire man, wounded at Chickamauga and having fought Comanches in Texas and Kiowas in Kansas, had simply grown old on the frontier. A tall, white-haired man with a drooping white mustache, he walked hunched over like a crane with painful knees. No one expected much from him except to see that the prisoners were fed and the jail was kept clean.

The new marshal tried to keep his sense of humor as nightly he faced the problem of dealing with fun-starved drovers in liquor with so much money in their pockets they thought they could buy the moon and ride it home.

If they couldn't buy it or ride it, they could shoot it, and every night a pack of riders would cut loose from the Red Dog

8

Saloon or the Drover's Rest and ride up and down First Street howling like a coyote reunion, blazing away at the sky, and keeping awake most townsmen who wanted to sleep.

"Hold her down, old hoss!" Marshal Cromwell yelled to a trio of sun-blackened men in new clothes who would be dead broke in another two days.

The whites of their eyes seemed to gleam like china cups against their gaunt, sunburned faces.

"Hold her down, boys," the young marshal called, still holding his smile.

"Ah'm ah tagger fum the canebrakes!"

"Ah'm a alligator from Bittercreek!"

"Ah'm a ring-tailed roarer from the prairies of the west!"

"I said, hold her down, buckaroos."

Young Cromwell was losing his patience and honest smile as the three cowboys froghopped and bucked their ponies up and down the street, blazing away at the sky with their single-action Colts.

"What's that you say, Marshal?" the shortest and ugliest one of the three yelled.

"I said hold her down or I'm goin' to lock you up."

"Lock me up? Me? Why, I'm the blue-eyed lynx of Whiskey Crossin', and it's my night to howl! Whooooeeeee!"

With that, the short cowboy snapped a shot which, though he meant it to be considerably higher than it was, whispered by Dave Cromwell's ear.

Dave's right hand flashed downward, palmed his six-gun, and on the rise, fired. The 128-grain lead ball caught the cowboy in the lower shoulder with such force he was blown out of the saddle and fell to the street.

"Drop the guns!" Dave yelled, aiming at the next rider, who had stopped his horse by his wounded comrade. The third one looked over his shoulder, set his spurs, and ran.

"Get him over to Doc Faris and then get out of town," the marshal said, his voice strained and high. "I'd lock you both up if the jail wasn't already full."

"Hell, why'd you shoot him?" the cowboy asked. "We wasn't hurtin' nothin'!"

"He took a shot at me and he's damned lucky he's not wolfbait."

"Need any help, Dave?" old Lou Wolford called from the office.

"Not yet, Lou," Dave answered. "Hold the fort."

Later that night two waddies from dif-

10

ferent outfits took a disliking to each other and went out in the street to settle their differences. Both were dead and hauled off to Tom Fancher's Fine Furniture and Funeral Parlor before daybreak.

So passed the night of April twenty-third.

Next day was Friday, press day for the *Ellsworth Record Republican Weekly*, and half the editorial page was taken up by Oakley Hunter, the editor, roaring about the violence in the streets.

Indeed most of the copper-bottomed citizens had had enough. By word of mouth throughout the day, they passed the word. At noon they met in the one-room schoolhouse and asked Eloise Abbott to extend the pupils' lunch time. Since the mayor was her large and portly father, Roy Abbott, she could hardly refuse.

After big Roy Abbott, owner of the General Mercantile, called the meeting to order, he counted twelve people, including Reverend P. G. Edenfield and himself.

"What do we want?" he asked the group. "Law and order, or madness and mayhem in the streets every night?"

They all agreed, except for some objection by Mickey Malone, proprietor of the Drover's Rest.

"Why don't the marshal arrest them troublemakers?" Wayne Askey, the harness maker, questioned, his pinched features forever in complaint.

"The jail is jammed full by ten o'clock every night," said cadaverous Carl Doran, owner of the Corner Café. "The whole thing is a mess."

Then came the babble of their complaints about the desecration of their up-and-coming town until Roy Abbott rapped on the teacher's desk with her hardwood yardstick.

"I suggest we put a sign at both entrances to town saying Ellsworth is a law and order town."

"And beware," joked George Philbrick, the barber, "or we'll shoot your pants off."

"Where's Pat Kimball?" banker Phil Meredith asked. "He ought to be here."

"He's always too busy down at the Ritz Hotel." Bert Gwinner, the liveryman in faded dungarees, grinned. "He never has time for anything except —"

"Careful, Bert . . ." George Philbrick laughed.

"You want a sign, or not?" Roy Abbott was losing his patience. "Something like 'You Break the Law, You Go to Jail.' "

"Carl said the jail is full every night," Reverend Edenfield said.

"Well then, put on it 'If You Don't Obey the Law, You Can Expect to Take the Consequences!' " Roy Abbott said strongly.

"Consequences?" Mickey Malone smiled. "I'll bet you two-to-one those Texas drovers can't read that big of a word."

"All right," Oakley Hunter said, scribbling on a pad of paper, " 'Welcome to Ellsworth. Obey the Laws or Pay the Price.' "

"That says it," said Tom Fancher of the Fine Furniture and Funeral, yawning. "Pardon me, I been up all night dressing bodies I'll never get paid for."

"Agreed?" Roy Abbott asked.

The members of the council hardly thought it was a fateful decision that would affect each one's life in some tragic way, and joined in a quick "Aye!"

"Put up these signs, Charlie," Roy Abbott said to the carpenter and wheelwright, Charlie Damker, who could also double as a painter. "And send us the bill."

"I'll get right at it," Charlie Damker replied, and he followed the rest of the council out into the schoolyard, where they dispersed to their various businesses on First Street.

The jail was emptied of overnight guests and cleaned and ready for those coming in that night. Deputy Lou Wolford swept out the office and the boardwalk in front and then cleaned and oiled his guns.

Some sorry punchers in new flannel shirts and dungarees found themselves with massive headaches and empty pockets, and without remorse, they headed south to find work for another year, while new crews moved their herds into the huge pens by the tracks, took their pay, and came into town, dirty, bone-tired, scruffy, short-tempered, unencumbered, and comparatively rich.

Some paused for a bath at the back of the barber shop, but others, more in a hurry to flush the trail dust from their pipes, rambled into the Red Dog or the Drover's Rest, bought a bottle of clear whiskey stained amber with chewing tobacco, and proceeded to go crazy. The babble in the afternoon grew to a roaring crescendo in the night. Men who had been calm, tight-mouthed, hardworking professional cattlemen for the past year suddenly became raucous, howling savages clutching at the sporting girls in wild stomping dances, staggering from one saloon to the other, firing off a shot for joy occasionally, and raising hell in general, no matter what the signs at the edge of town said.

Red Swinton, a hand from the Wineglass crew that had been paid off the week before, found himself broke, alone, and only half drunk. He could probably mooch enough drinks to get through the night, but he knew from experience his hoo-raw was over and that he was doomed to spend another year chasing cattle.

With that dismal prospect in the back of his head, he studied a handsome steeldust gelding that had been tied to the hitchrail for several hours.

He reasoned that if he had to ride back to Texas, he'd ought to do it in style, and as there seemed to be no owner of the powerful horse, why not just help himself?

He knew full well why not, knew it was a hanging offense, but being half drunk and mad because he had nothing to show for the money he'd spent so soon, he decided he'd be damned if he did and damned if he didn't.

His bleary mind settled, he paused at the hitchrail and furtively undid the simple rein hitch, then stepped under the rail, gathered both reins in his left hand, and mounted the steeldust.

Red wanted to ride out slow and easy,

but once aboard, panic won out, and he dug his spurs into the steeldust's flanks and sent him roaring out of town like a load of buckshot.

Being unfamiliar with the country, he rode south until he thought he was safe, then he dismounted near a small creek, picketed the steeldust, and went to sleep.

He was rudely awakened by a half-dozen cowboys and Marshal Dave Cromwell, each with a weapon pointed at his head.

"Let's hang him right here," a lantern-jawed cowboy said.

"You identify this horse as your property?"

"I got the bill of sale," the cowboy said. "That enough to hang him?"

"Probably, but we'll let the judge decide," Marshal Cromwell said.

"I ain't waitin' around for no judge," the cowboy said. "I say string him up right now."

"You stole this horse?" Cromwell asked Swinton.

"I did, but I was drunk."

"You can explain it to the judge," Cromwell said.

"I'm right sorry I did it, and I give you my word I'd never do it again."

"It don't make any difference, drunk or

16

sober, a horse thief is still buzzard bait where I come from," the steeldust's owner came back hotly.

"Let me handle it, boys," the young marshal said quietly. "You've got your horse back, and I've got my man."

In that way Red Swinton was lodged in the Ellsworth jail and remained there day after day while the drunks came in the night and left in the morning, a type of torture as bad as most anything a savage Indian could dream up.

Red's cronies were already gone south, he was a stranger in town, and he had no money. Moreover, he was despised by everyone as only horse thieves can be despised. For committing one rash act, his life was ruined. His only value to society now was to show by example that stealing horses didn't pay.

This affair was not overlooked by the citizens of Ellsworth, who regarded it as a deliberate attempt to flout the law in spite of their announcements that lawbreakers would pay the price.

Resentment among the inner circle — composed of about a dozen professional men, storekeepers, and craftsmen — accelerated as the debauchery on their streets accelerated. They didn't overly blame their marshal. At considerable risk to his own hide, he filled the jail, and still hundreds of wild-eyed cowboys paid no more attention than a runaway horse pays attention to the bit in his teeth.

When the citizens went home for dinner, their wives ragged at them about this lawless hellhole, and what were the men of Ellsworth — men or mice?

What about the children? It wasn't safe for the little ones to even play outside.

"Build a bigger jail!" Oakley Hunter thundered in his editorial the next Friday. "Lock them up like caged beasts until they see the error of their ways."

"Who has money enough for a big, new, fancy jail?" Roy Abbott answered for all of them.

"Tax the saloons, they're the ones making the profit."

"In a pig's ass," responded Mick Malone and Ed Rowan, who were busy harvesting a bumper crop from the willing cowpunchers.

"They've got to be stopped. They've taken over our town and decent people won't settle here," Phil Meredith the banker complained.

"Put gates at each end of town," Reverend P. G. Edenfield suggested, which only added to the gathering cloud of frustration, because all of them wanted the river of easy money that accompanied the Texas cattle to the railhead.

Smoky Hill Cemetery became a familiar place.

Now every citizen, even Reverend Edenfield, carried a sidearm somewhere on his body, and women refused to go out into the streets to do their shopping, sending their husbands instead.

Young Jim Maclanahan, a lanky lad of eighteen from Kentucky, rode across country near Blackwolf Creek. When he heard a shot a half a mile on up the trail, he checked his pony and considered whether to go forward or swing around, and as he thought about it, he saw a rattlesnake coiled by the trail. His instinctive response was to haul out the heavy old Dragoon six-gun and shoot.

The snake writhed in torn pieces, its head gone. He scabbarded the Dragoon and proceeded on up the trail.

Over a low rise he came across a four-year-old steer that had been shot between the eyes. It bore the Elkhorn brand and was still twitching. He dismounted to study the tracks. Two men had shot the steer. When they heard his shot, they ran.

It was simple — he'd surprised a pair of meat hunters.

Now the proper thing to do would be to inform whoever ran the Elkhorn Ranch that he had a problem.

He was saved that journey by the arrival of two riders from the east coming at full tilt with six-guns drawn.

Jim Maclanahan had sense enough to put his hands up high.

"Talk about red-handed!" the old man said. "Get his gun, Rafe."

"You fellas from the Elkhorn Ranch?" Jim Maclanahan asked, unafraid.

"I own it," the old man said, "and my son here helps run it. Why'd you kill my beef? Just for a hunk of round steak?"

"I didn't kill it," Jim said, as Rafe sniffed at the barrel of the Dragoon.

"Fresh fired." He nodded to his father. "We finally got him."

"There was two of them. You can see their tracks," Jim Maclanahan said.

But the tracks had been obliterated by the boots of the son, and there was no evidence to prove Jim Maclanahan innocent and plenty to prove him guilty.

"Shall we whip him off the range or just hang him?"

"Wait, son," the old man said, "the other

20

times there was two of them ridin' shod horses."

"That's right," the son said, and turning to young Jim, smashed him across the face with the back of his hand.

"Where's your partner?"

"I'm a loner," Jim Maclanahan said. "I don't have a partner and I didn't kill your beef."

The son smacked him again and said, "I want an answer."

"I told you true. I don't steal."

"Wait," the old man said, "don't bust your knuckles on him. We'll take him in to Ellsworth and let the marshal handle it."

"I think I can beat it out of him," the son replied, balling his fist.

"No. I got a feelin' I don't like," the old man said, and he hunched his shoulders as if a shivering wind had blown down his backbone.

Marshal Dave Cromwell shook his head when the Elkhorn pair brought in the youth. "That boy's too young to be out shootin' cows on the range."

"We caught him in the act. It's the way the world is nowadays," the old man said. "Maybe he'll talk to you. I'd like to find his partner."

After the old man and his son had gone,

Dave asked the tall youth what he had to say.

"I didn't do it," Jim Maclanahan drawled respectfully. "If you please, Marshal, I'd like to write a letter to my ma to let her know where I am."

Dave found paper and pen and passed them through the bars and asked enviously, "How'd you learn to write?"

"My ma was a schoolmarm before she married," Jim Maclanahan replied, and he composed a brief letter to his mother back up in Hornbeak, Kentucky. When he finished, he asked for an envelope and a stamp and gave Dave three copper pennies to cover the expense.

"I'll post it for you," Dave said, putting the letter in his breast pocket. "I'm goin' up the street anyways."

"Thank you kindly, sir," Jim Maclanahan said, and Marshal Dave Cromwell looked into the boy's dark eyes and knew he was innocent.

Dave walked to the next block to the square-built one-room schoolhouse from which the youngsters were now running as if they'd been confined for a week instead of a few hours. Shirttails and pigtails flying, the boys and girls raced for home, hooting and yodeling as they ran.

On the steps, watching her charges run free, stood Eloise Abbott, her dark hair curling gently about her own happy face, which was distinguished by high cheekbones and straight-across eyebrows that couldn't conceal the deep blue of her eyes. Her generous mouth was framed in a wide smile of pleasure as if she'd worked hard, finished the job, and was proud of herself.

"Howdy, Miss Eloise," Paul said, touching his hat brim. "You look as pleased as a treeful of bluebirds."

"The kids are so wonderful," she said. "They want to learn everything in one day."

"I'm like that too, but I'm not a kid anymore," he said, starting to blush just from being near the pretty girl.

"I'm sure you could teach me a lot of things about horses and cows, grass and water, camp cooking and ranch life."

"Heck, everybody knows those things. What I'd like for you to think about is maybe, come winter, when the law business cools down, maybe you could teach me readin' and writin'."

"Of course," she responded, "but what brought this urge for learning on?"

"Well, ma'am, I just seen a boy hardly a man yet write his ma a letter without having to puzzle on how to make the words, and I figure maybe someday I can write my folks in Texas and tell them not to worry, I'm doin' fine," he smiled.

"I'll trade you, Dave. You teach me how to rope a calf, and I'll teach you how to write."

Again Dave blushed shyly, as she smiled and put her hand out.

"That's a deal, ma'am," he said, shaking her hand gently.

From down the street came the blood-curdling cry of an imitation Comanche and the booming of a six-gun.

"They're startin' early. Looks like it'll be a long night," he said, turning away quickly, yet still remembering to touch his hat before heading down the street to collar a cowboy loaded already with over-much forty rod.

Firing into the air, the cowboy stood in the stirrups, lifted the bay gelding up on its hind legs, and squalled like a puma, his eyes rolling white. In a moment he was joined by another rowdy puncher who waved his stained and battered Stetson, revealing a pallid skull bald as a hardboiled egg.

"C'mon, Curly," the bald man's cohort on the rearing bay yelled, "let's tree us a town!"

Curly's Colt .45 flashed blue in his hand as he raised it over his head and spurred his horse down the street with a caterwaul capable of disturbing the sleepers on Smoky Hill.

"Hold it!" Dave yelled.

"C'mon, Frank, let's see if the new marshal can dance!" Curly grinned and whirled his horse back the way he'd come, firing into the dirt near Dave's feet.

"Curly, dim dammit, stop!" Dave yelled.

The puncher named Frank on the bay horse followed along and charged Dave.

Dave sidestepped to the boardwalk as bullets peppered the dirt. Hardly hearing a faint whimper behind him, he drew and aimed his Navy Colt right on Frank's wide forehead.

"Don't shoot! I'm empty!" Frank yelled, suddenly sobered up. Throwing the empty six-shooter to the ground, he raised his hands high.

Dave's aim went over to a crestfallen Curly, who threw his empty revolver down and lifted his hands.

Behind and down the boardwalk, Dave heard the small cry again.

"If you move an inch, I'll drop you," he said, and he turned around to look at a baby doll lying near a thin packing case in front of the Mercantile.

Puzzled for a second, he advanced slowly and then saw a small hand reach for the doll just as Lou Wolford hobbled across the street.

"Take 'em in, Lou," he said quietly and kneeled by the box, moving it aside to reveal a little girl with blonde pigtails.

She wore a red skirt and blouse, so that at first he couldn't quite believe it was her blood seeping across the boardwalk.

"Get Doc!" he yelled, kneeling beside the little girl.

She had been shot through the body. Not daring to move her, Dave touched her hair gently and said, "It's all right, Kathy, it's all right. Doc's coming."

"Mama —" little Kathy cried weakly.

"She's comin' too. Just hold on awhile."

Lou Wolford locked up Curly Dorn and Frank Rostetter unaware that they might have caused a terrible accident.

Little Kathy was carried to the doctor's office where her mother, Hope Doran, crouched beside her, and her father, Carl, paced the floor.

Doc kept shaking his head, but he wouldn't say a plain out yes or no.

"She's alive," was all he'd say.

"Must've been a ricochet," Dave said to Carl Doran.

"Don't say it was an accident, Dave." Cadaverous Carl Doran glared at the young lawman. "Those two are going to swing."

"The judge should be in tomorrow. We can wait until then and keep a clear conscience," Dave said softly. "I'd not like anything unlawful happening to my prisoners."

"I told them you were too young for this job. Why didn't you shoot them off their horses before they ever got started?" Carl Doran cried out angrily.

"Easy does it, Carl." Dave tried to calm the man. "We need to think right and say some prayers."

"Don't you understand?" Carl Doran's voice rose. "She's all we have! There won't be any more!"

"She's goin' to pull through," Dave said.

He'd seen the wound — he knew he was lying, and he left.

# 2

As Marshal Dave Cromwell stepped outside into First Street, he noticed the hitchrails were nearly cleared of horses and that the usual raucous hooting of crazed drovers had been replaced by the mournful keening of the prairie wind blowing down the empty street.

The punchers had heard about little Kathy and either from fear or from shame had gone back to their camps, where they'd think on this tragic afternoon and ride the night watch making a song . . .

> "In a town way up in Kansas,
> Ellsworth by name,
> My little sweetheart was playing
> A baby doll game . . .
>> Roll on, roll on,
>> Roll on, little dogies, roll on,
>>> roll on. . . ."

Dave crossed the street to the jail and found old Lou lighting a lamp for the evening. To the rear, down a short hall, was the large single cell that contained four bunks and the prisoners.

"How is she?" Lou asked, settling the globe over the flame.

"I pray she lives, but a .45 ball makes a godawful big hole."

"Murder?"

"Maybe. Even if it was an accident, the judge will hang them. Carl thinks I should have shot them out of the saddle, but I know old Curly. He's the quietest cowboy, most of the time."

"Except when he tanks up on white lightning."

"Heck, he showed me once how to catch a calf with a figure eight. I couldn't just shoot him, because he didn't know what he was doin'."

"Betwixt you and me, the Dorans hadn't ought to let her play in the street. It ain't right," old Lou muttered thoughtfully.

"Still, the streets belong to everybody and we're supposed to keep 'em safe."

"I reckon I'm talkin' too much. Times like these, Dave, best be extra careful." Lou lighted his pipe. "Folks remember."

"Nothin' like this has ever happened before. It's hard to know how to handle it."

"Better hope no hotheaded spellbinder starts talkin' about quick justice and a necktie party," Lou muttered.

"These folks are too level-headed for lynchin'," Dave said. "They know the judge'll be here Monday."

"What I see is these folks all makin' a livin' off the drovers. Now, when you sup with the devil, you better have a long spoon. I don't mind much what these folks think, but I do mind sacrificin' the little children just for a few dollars extra profit."

"That's why they hire us, Lou. We're supposed to protect them."

"I know." Lou puffed his pipe aglow. "You do a good job of it too, but I'm sayin' you invite a bull into your china shop, somethin's goin' to get broke."

"We got to do better," Dave said. "I reckon the only way we can stop such things is to tell 'em to leave their guns to home or else check 'em with us."

"Good idea. These rannies think they was born with a tallywhacker twixt their legs and a six-gun on their hip."

"I'm goin' to ask the city council to pass a law that gets the guns off the street," Dave Cromwell said.

"You can't enforce it, Dave."

"Look, Lou, I didn't say it would be easy, and I may have to shoot a few of the worst of the knotheads, but word will spread on down the trail and through the camps that Ellsworth is not a helltown anymore."

"Makes me nervous as a duck in the desert, it bein' so quiet out there." Lou went to the door. "Maybe I better mosey on down the street for a look-see."

Lou looked out the doorway into the night. A dim light illuminated the street from the windows of the Red Dog and the Drover's Rest, otherwise an eerie dark silence pervaded the town, as if a shroud had been pulled over its streets and buildings.

"Somethin' goin' on I don't like," the old man said, going out.

"Let me know," Dave said, going to the gun rack and checking the heavy octagonal-barreled Winchesters.

He thought he'd ask Charlie Damker to build him a cabinet full of pigeonholes where he could store the revolvers of men coming into town armed. Have numbers, and give the man a little chit so's he could get the right gun back.

It would be extra work and troublesome, but at least there wouldn't be any more wild shooting. Talk to Roy Abbott tomorrow. Cowboys, like Lou said, wouldn't like it, but they'd get used to it after a while or they could go someplace else.

The only loss to the town would be a

slowdown in the selling of cartridges.

From the gun rack he went down the hall and saw the four prisoners staring at him through the bars. High up on the back wall, a small barred window let the air move through.

"Everythin' all right?" he asked.

Curly Dorn and Frank Rostetter were standing side by side, holding on to the bars, the color of their faces pale as putty, their eyes downcast.

"Reckon we're in the soup," Frank Rostetter said.

"Likely," Dave said.

"I just wish there was some way of undoin' it," Curly Dorn murmured.

"Best thing you can say it was an accident," Dave said. "I don't hold that part of you tryin' to devil me against you."

"It's that goddamned hi-test liquor," Red Swinton said. "It makes you do things you wouldn't otherwise."

"But everybody knows what it does, and yet they can't wait to pay out their money for a drink of it."

"Amen to that," Frank Rostetter said.

"Goddamn it," Curly murmured and clasped his hands together, a hint of moisture in his eyes as he reproached himself again.

"Well, we done it," Frank Rostetter said, angry at himself, knowing there was nothing left to say.

"I pray she lives," Curly said. "I don't care what they do to me, I just don't want that on my conscience."

"I mailed your letter, Jim," Dave said to the tall youth sitting on the edge of a bunk.

"Thank you kindly," Jim Maclanahan replied. "I mentioned in there that you're just doin' your duty and you been square with me."

"I'm goin' to learn readin' and writin'," Dave said.

"Well, it's not so hard once you get the hang of it. Ma taught me from the Bible. She said, that way I got double duty." Jim Maclanahan smiled. "Now, wouldn't she be some surprised to see me in here."

"I doubt the judge'll bind you over," Dave said. "I can tell him what I think."

"What do you think?"

"I think you didn't kill that steer, and if you had, you wouldn't do it again."

"That's fair." The youth smiled, his dark eyes content. "I aim to get back to Kentucky, but there ain't no big wind apushin' me."

"Tell him I won't never steal a horse again," Red Swinton said.

Dave looked at him. "I don't know. Maybe you would, maybe you wouldn't. I kind of think you done it before, but you never got caught. Pretty soon you thought it was so easy, you didn't even worry about it."

The redheaded horse thief turned around and paced the floor without replying.

"Why's it so blamed quiet?" Curly Dorn burst out.

"Town's empty. Everybody went home," Dave said.

There was a long silence as they digested that piece of information.

"They're scared," Frank Rostetter growled.

"Scared of what?" Jim Maclanahan asked.

"Scared some of these town gents goin' to start haulin' out their pea shooters."

"I wouldn't blame 'em one damned bit neither," Frank Rostetter cursed angrily.

"I just pray to God she lives," Curly repeated again. "And, Lord, I ain't never prayed for nothin' in my whole life."

"I can remember when it sounded like a herd of longhorns stampedin' and a regular haze of gunsmoke hangin' over the street," Red Swinton said.

"No more," Dave said. "It's just a memory now."

"Oh, Lord." Curly leaned his face down

on his forearm, covering his eyes.

"Dave —"

The young marshal heard Lou call from the doorway.

"Yes."

"Mind comin' out here?"

Dave Cromwell walked down the hall into the office and saw Lou standing out on the boardwalk waiting.

"What is it?"

"I can't say," old Lou replied hoarsely, as if he'd lost his breath.

Dave went out the door and took one step on the boardwalk, when he saw a figure holding a shotgun against old Lou's bowed back. The figure had a white flour sack over his head with eye holes cut out.

"What . . ." Dave started to say, when a gun barrel came down on his head from behind.

Dave came to, lying in the corner of his office. It took him a moment of painful thinking to orient himself. He'd been coldcocked on the boardwalk — how had he gotten in here? With his eyes still closed, he heard voices that he knew, voices of the townspeople. He tried to rise and found that his ankles were tied together. He shifted his arms and discovered his arms were handcuffed behind his back. He tried to speak and felt a new bandanna tied across his mouth like a bridle bit, permitting him to breathe but not to speak.

Why hadn't they blindfolded him?

Because they wanted him to see, he managed to think in spite of the recurring lightning flashes and painful thunder roaring through his head.

Why?

Through a shimmering haze as his vision cleared he saw a crowd of men, all wearing flour sacks over their heads. Maybe you could swear that worsted suit belonged to Oakley Hunter, or maybe you could say those paint-spattered dungarees fit Charlie Damker, but you'd have a heck of a time proving it. Each man's identity was known, and yet no one could swear in a court of law as to the real truth of it.

Turning his head, he saw old Lou trussed to the office chair. At least they hadn't hit the old man over the head.

He understood then that this was all a deliberately planned action.

Lou looked over at him and saw that he was conscious.

"Little Kathy died a half-hour ago," he spoke in an undertone.

So there would be a hanging, Dave

thought. They wouldn't wait for the judge. They wanted their vengeance right now.

"Open it up."

The voice of bulky Roy Abbott was unmistakable.

A shrunken little man who had to be Wayne Askey, the harness maker, inserted the big key and turned the lock.

"All right, you men, all of you, come on out of there," Roy Abbott said, holding a ten-gauge shotgun aimed at the prisoners.

"Look —" Frank Rostetter said angrily, "it was an accident. We ain't makin' any excuses, but we sure didn't set out to kill a little girl."

"She is dead from a bullet fired by one of you!" the voice of Phil Meredith the banker declared.

"I want a jury trial," Curly Dorn said strongly. "I don't mind dyin' for doin' a crazy thing, but I want it legal."

"You have nothing to say about it," said Del Morton, the Delmonico's restaurant owner. "C'mon. All of you! Out!"

"We put up the sign," Oakley Hunter said, "said you'd pay the price, now you goin' to pay."

"Not me!" Red Swinton burst out. "I didn't even see a sign!"

"All of you." Charlie Damker.

"I'm bettin' all four will pee their pants," Mick Malone, the Red Dog owner, declared. "I'll bet five hundred dollars on it."

"Not the boy," old Lou called out.

"Shut up, you old devil," Bert Gwinner, the liveryman, snarled. "This ain't your show. You all had your chance, and look what happened."

Dave Cromwell struggled vainly against his bonds and then slumped back in the corner. The hooded men were partly right. Some of this was his fault. He should have pushed for a no-gun law a month ago, he just hadn't thought it necessary. He'd thought he could handle any gunman in town and hadn't reckoned on a child playing with her doll on the street. No excuses.

The tall youth was crouched on the bottom bunk, staring out at the masked men with curiosity, as if he had just discovered a new kind of animal.

"Why you gents wearing them flour sacks?" he asked. "Everybody but me must know who you are."

"Silence!" Roy Abbott boomed.

"Seems kind of foolish to me, is all," the youth drawled. "Growed men hidin' their faces —"

"I said, shut up!" Abbott's voice commanded.

"Get them out of there," shouted Phil Meredith, the banker.

Bert Gwinner, George Philbrick, Del Morton, and Wayne Askey crowded into the cell, encircled the prisoners, forced them out into the hall and on into the office.

The youth Jim Maclanahan paled when he saw Dave Cromwell bound and gagged in the corner and old Lou tied to the chair.

He'd had some hope for help, but he saw the handwriting on the wall. There would be no help except from his own doing, and already his hands were bound behind his back.

"All right, we're goin' to have the trial," Abbott declared. "You four are charged with committing crimes in Ellsworth County. How do you plead?"

"I'm guilty," Curly said bitterly. "Sure, I'm guilty, but I don't want a bunch of city slickers puttin' me down."

"I'm guilty of causin' an accident, I guess," Frank Rostetter said angrily, "and if it was my fault, I'll pay for it, but who really knows whose fault it was?"

"You," Oakley Hunter pointed at Red Swinton.

"I didn't do nothin' worth hangin' for," Red said levelly. "I got drunk, I admit to that, and I did a foolish thing, I admit to that, but who ain't done the same thing?"

"You?" Tom Fancher, the furniture salesman and embalmer, demanded of Jim Maclanahan.

"I'm innocent," the boy said simply. "The marshal here knows it, if you'll let him talk."

"That's enough!" Roy Abbott waved his shotgun. "Now we have twelve jurors good and true and I want each one on the record. How do you find these men, innocent or guilty?"

"Guilty." Carl Doran spoke first, his voice shaking.

"Guilty," Oakley Hunter said loudly.

"Guilty," said Wayne Askey, the harness maker.

"Guilty," snapped Del Morton of Delmonico's.

"I'm not sure . . ." came the voice of young Reverend P. G. Edenfield, "that the Lord gave us this right. . . ."

"Say it, damn it," Roy Abbott bellowed.

"Guilty," the preacher said weakly, his soft features sagging.

"Guilty," said Bert Gwinner, the sprunglegged liveryman.

"Guilty as charged." Phil Meredith nodded judiciously.

"Guilty," Tom Fancher intoned in a

practiced melancholy voice.

"Guilty as hell!" Mick Malone shouted.

"Time's a wastin'," Charlie Damker said.

"All right, gentlemen, I, too, find the prisoners guilty as charged, and they are hereby sentenced by mutual agreement to death by hanging."

"So help them God," Reverend Edenfield, now caught up in the fever, intoned solemnly.

"Whereaway?" Oakley Hunter asked.

"Find a place," Wayne Askey said.

"But where?"

"Heck, I don't know — from a tree, I reckon," Del Morton said, his words slurred.

"There ain't a tree that big in all Ellsworth," said George Philbrick, giggling nervously.

There was a silence as the unforeseen problem hit the hooded jurors, and each went through his mind trying to think of a suitable place for the execution.

"You want 'em hangin' from the roof of the Mercantile?" Tom Fancher suggested. "It's close to the Funeral Parlor."

"No, it won't do," Roy Abbott said.

"We need a place that will set an example for all the other outlaws coming up the trail," Oakley Hunter declared.

"There's the railroad trestle east of town," Charlie Damker said.

"That's it!" Mick Malone said. "They can pee their pants right down to the river!"

"You sonofabitch —" Frank Rostetter lunged at Malone, but was stopped by a double-barreled goose gun pressed against his chin.

"It's a long ways out there to walk," Tom Fancher said.

"I'll get my dray," Bert Gwinner said, and he left the office, limping on his sprung leg.

"Shall we pray?" Reverend Edenfield asked softly in the momentary silence.

"No!" Carl Doran said. "If there was a God to pray to, he wouldn't have let Kathy die this way."

"Please believe me," Jim Maclanahan said softly, "I'm innocent of any crime."

"Shut up," Roy Abbott growled. "Move them outside where folks can see them."

More to keep busy than anything else, the men jostled the prisoners out the door and into the street.

Marshal Dave Cromwell kicked at the desk with both feet in protest.

"Cut his legs loose," Roy Abbott said, "and bring the old man too. We want everybody to see justice done."

George Philbrick stepped forward with his penknife and cut the bonds around Dave's boots and the cord tying Lou Wolford to the chair.

"Listen, you two, we already agreed that you can be nothing more than silent witnesses to this court. Understood?" Roy Abbott said.

Lou remained silent, and Dave Cromwell, with eyes blazing, shook his head.

"Very well, let us proceed," Roy Abbott said heavily, and he went into the street with the others.

When Bert Gwinner arrived driving a large dray with short sideboards pulled by a pair of strong Missouri mules, the prisoners were forced to climb up into the scarred oak bed, along with four guards and the two peace officers. The others, paired up in buggies and buckboards, followed the dray out past the church and school to the railroad bridge spanning the Smoky Hill River.

Each vehicle carried a bullseye lantern which marked their melancholy procession through the night. The moon was nearly dark and on the wane.

The timbered truss bridge rose twenty feet over the river, which allowed enough height to meet the spring flooding.

The ties had been planked over so railroad workers could walk safely and even bring up a wagon of hardware if necessary, although it was considered too dangerous by most because of the possibility of an oncoming train.

For this reason, although the next train was not scheduled to pass through eastbound until after daybreak, they stopped their conveyances at the foot of the bridge and, carrying their lanterns, marched up to the high point of the bridge. A low railing of imported pine logs protected each side of the bridge and there was plenty of room for eighteen men.

Their boots clumped on the planks as the guards crowded their prisoners up the elevation, followed by the rest of the jury and the pinioned lawmen.

When they had gathered at the top of the span, Roy Abbott said, "I guess we're ready . . ."

"All we need is some strong twine," Phil Meredith said.

"I don't know —" muttered Oakley Hunter.

"Where are the ropes?" Roy Abbott asked coldly.

There was no answer.

Stabbing a finger at Wayne Askey,

Abbott said, "You were supposed to furnish the ropes."

"I guess I forgot, in all the excitement." Askey set his jaw like a steel trap. "You want to make somethin' out of it?"

"Take my buggy and hurry," Roy Abbott commanded angrily.

"Please, gentlemen," Jim Maclanahan spoke softly, "I don't belong here. If you kill me, you'll have killed the wrong man. That's murder, and that's against the law of God and man."

"You have been convicted and sentenced to death by hanging. We'll give you time to talk before you swing," growled Phil Meredith, the short, paunchy banker, before anyone could consider what the boy had just said.

"Anybody got a bottle?" Del Morton asked. "I feel a cold coming on."

"Lucky I brought a bottle of my special reserve." Mick Malone laughed and hefted an unlabeled quart bottle full of more or less clear whiskey.

Del Morton took the bottle, uncorked it, slipped the neck up under his hood, and drank.

Coughing and swearing, he handed the bottle back to Malone. "That's sure good."

"You boys want a little nose paint before

45

you go over?" Malone proffered the bottle to the prisoners.

"I'm here because of a bottle of that," Curly Dorn said.

Frank Rostetter shook his head angrily.

"Hell, yes, let 'er buck!" Red Swinton laughed, and he leaned his face forward so that Malone could pour a draught down his throat.

"Many thanks," Red said when he got his breath back.

"You, boy?"

"Not that stuff."

"You're used to the pure quill, are you?" Malone sneered.

"My brother back in Kentucky makes such a sweet whiskey you can sip it out of the copper worm," the boy replied.

"Gimme a jolt of that." George Philbrick's voice covered what the boy was saying, and no one paid any attention as the barber tipped the bottle under his mask and took a swig.

"Well, godalmighty, don't drink it all!" Malone laughed and took a drink himself. "Ain't anybody want a piece of my five hundred dollars they all pee their pants?"

"You bastard," Frank Rostetter snarled, and Malone backhanded him hard.

"Watch your mouth, cowboy. We may

just hang you by your pizzle first."

"Here he comes," Tom Fancher said, looking off at the road where a bullseye lamp marked the buggy's coming. "Let's get it over and done with."

"About time," grumbled Oakley Hunter. "I'm about set to change my mind."

"There's no goin' back now," Carl Doran said harshly.

Wayne Askey came huffing and puffing up the incline with four coils of new manila half-inch rope.

"There you go," he said gruffly. "They'll do."

"Can you tie the knots?" Roy Abbott asked, trying to maintain some sense of decorum.

"Sure. I can tie a hangman's knot in my sleep," Askey cackled. "I while away the time making hangman's knots instead of playin' mumblety-peg like the rest of you."

Dave Cromwell strained futilely at the handcuffs but accomplished nothing. He thought Askey must have had some drinks on the way back, the way he was chattering on, or maybe he was just talking to cover up his nervousness. It didn't matter. What mattered was to stop this crime before it went any further. If he could just talk, he'd tell them what he thought. He'd tell them he'd report every damned one of them to the governor and have each and every one's hide hanging on the fence no matter how long it took. He'd tell them they couldn't have law and order unless they were unblemished themselves, that you can't have law and order if there's corruption anywhere along the line, especially at the top.

In the awkward silence as they waited, men shifted their feet and squirmed inside, dreading the moment of commitment.

"Look," Malone called out a little drunkenly, "I'll give you odds. I'll give you two-to-one that they pee their pants."

"All of them, or some of them?" Del Morton laughed. "Why don't we take down their pants and make sure what they got?"

"I'll bet you any amount that this here Frank Rostetter will, and that skinheaded Curly Dorn, he does too," Malone persisted.

"Jesus God," Rostetter muttered, "I'd as liefer die as live in a world of sick skunks."

"I'm with you, Frank," Curly said disgustedly.

"Gentlemen, please —" Roy Abbott said, holding up his hand, "it is not seemly here. We're acting in the cause of justice, not as a Roman circus."

"There you go," announced Wayne Askey, carrying the four nooses to the prisoners and tossing them at their feet, "all the chokers you need."

"Hang the sonsabitches," Bert Gwinner said.

" 'Hang 'em all, the big and the small. Hang 'em all, the long and the tall, and if they're still in pain, hang 'em all over again . . .' " chanted George Philbrick, rolling his eyes and grinning.

"That's enough! Will somebody adjust the nooses under each prisoner's ear and secure the end to the rail," Roy Abbott asked.

George Philbrick, Bert Gwinner, Carl Doran, and Charlie Damker moved forward and proceeded to fix the nooses and secure the ends around the low log railing.

"This'll teach you some respect," crowed the wizened Charlie Damker.

"Very well. We are ready."

"Let this be a lesson to all men," Phil Meredith said.

"I'm not so sure," Oakley Hunter said weakly.

"Repent your sins!" Reverend Edenfield begged.

Ignoring him, Roy Abbott proceeded, "By the power invested in me by the mem-

49

bers of this jury, who are forever sworn to secrecy, I hereby ask that the preacher say a prayer as we carry out this execution."

"Our Father who art in heaven, hallowed be thy name. Thy kingdom come, thy will be done, on earth as it is in heaven —"

"Curly Dorn, have you any last words?"

"I just want to say I'm sorry about the little girl, don't know her name . . ."

"Kathy Doran," Carl Doran said huskily. "May you all fry in hell."

"Believe me, we didn't mean for it to happen."

"Thy kingdom come, thy will be done on earth as it is in heaven —"

"Die!" Roy Abbott abruptly shouldered Curly Dorn over the side. The rope squeaked as it stretched, and they heard Curly's neck bones pop.

"Give us this day our daily bread, and forgive us our trespasses —"

"Frank Rostetter, have you any last words?"

"I hope you fry in hell!" Frank Rostetter yelled and jumped. "You sonsa—"

"As we forgive those who trespass against us. Lead us not into temptation —"

"Red, you're next."

"Look, I didn't do nothin'! I just had some bad luck."

Roy Abbott bumped him, and he whimpered for a short second as he went over.

"But deliver us from evil —"

"You, what's your name?"

"Jim Maclanahan, sir."

"Have you any last words?"

"Yes, sir. I would like to say that you folks are making a bad mistake that will cost you everything." Jim Maclanahan stood straight as a ramrod and spoke without fear or anger. "I'm not begging you for my life, I'm begging you for yours . . ."

"and deliver us from evil —"

"Push him!" Carl Doran cried.

"Wait!" Oakley Hunter said, but too late.

The rope squeaked and the bones snapped.

Mick Malone clambered down by the railing and swung his bullseye lamp down toward the swinging bodies.

"I can't see!" he cried out in mock dismay. "Next time hang 'em with a shorter rope —"

"For thine is the kingdom and the power and the glory forevermore. Amen. . . ."

# 3

Phil Meredith was leaning over, whispering to Roy Abbott behind the counter near the cash drawer, when Dave Cromwell stepped inside the store.

"Well, good morning, Dave!" Abbott beamed, his little eyes measuring and calculating. "How are you this morning?"

"Morning, Marshal." Meredith nodded and stepped aside.

"What are you goin' to do about those four bodies?" Dave asked bluntly.

Abbott looked at the cold-eyed marshal and without a flicker of wonder or deceit on his face, said, "What bodies?"

"If you jokers think I'm goin' to play the toy soldier for you, you got another think comin'."

"I don't know what you mean, Dave." Abbott's voice was mild and persuasive.

"There are twelve murderers in this town now, cold-blooded killers who should be hangin' out there from the bridge."

"I'd be careful making accusations. You might find yourself looking for work." Phil

Meredith's frosty eyes bulged like an angry tom turkey's.

Dave Cromwell unpinned the brass star on his left breast pocket and tossed it on the counter.

"Come out in the street and talk some more." Cromwell's own eyes were like electric sparks charged with power.

"Calm down, Dave. Don't do anything you'll be sorry for. My daughter seems to think you have a future here."

"Leave Eloise out of this. I'm talkin' about justice."

"Justice was done in full," Phil Meredith, the paunchy banker, said.

"And you're both goin' to pay in full too, believe me!"

"Are you threatening us?"

"I'm sayin' all twelve of you are going to swing if I have anythin' to say about it. That's a promise."

"That's a threat and I'm a witness," Meredith snarled.

"Now, now, no point in making matters worse. Bygones will be bygones," Roy Abbott said smoothly, an oily smile puckered in the jowls. "I hear you been down at the telegraph office, Dave . . ."

"That's my business. I just come to tell you you're goin' to pay — the hard way," Dave said bleakly.

"You'd best not stay in Ellsworth," Abbott said. "Twelve honest men might think you're hangin' material too."

"There isn't one man in that unholy crew that would face me, including you, you gutless bastard."

Dave Cromwell strode out the door and down the boardwalk to the jail, angry at the town, the whole world, and himself.

"C'mon, Lou," he said to the old man standing in the doorway of the marshal's office. "We got us a job."

"I don't have a job, Dave. I just left my badge on the desk."

"Good man." Dave smiled at the forlorn old man. He knew what it had cost Lou to cut off his only security in a place where there was no work for cripples or oldtimers.

"I won't work for any of them," Lou said firmly. "But I hate to leave the town without some sort of law."

"I sent a wire to the U.S. Marshal's office in Topeka this morning early," Dave said. "I told 'em the story and that I was finished."

"That's about all we can do then. Now I've got to look around for a rich widow."

"You can help me out at the ranch," Dave said, "but right now, we're goin' to try to do somethin' decent."

"Buryin' 'em has been on my mind."

"First we need the dray and four coffins, then the undertaker and the preacher."

"Let's leave the preacher out." Lou tugged at his long white mustache.

"Don't get so riled up, Lou."

"I tell you, I won't forget that fork-tongued sonofabitch."

Bert Gwinner stared at them, his fleshy face grey and puffy.

"The dray?"

He was about to say no when he noticed Dave Cromwell's fist balled up like a burned rock and the old man behind him with his hand on the walnut butt of his Colt.

"Take it," he muttered and turned away.

Driving the heavy wagon up Second Street, Dave stopped the mule team in front of Charlie Damker's shop and handed the reins to Lou. "I'll just be a minute."

Climbing down from the wagon, Dave entered the wheel and carpenter shop that smelled of freshly dressed wood. He found Charlie Damker in the back of the shop, fitting hickory spokes into a wheel rim.

"I want four coffins."

"Fine. They're ten dollars apiece."

"The city council will pay, one way or another." Dave noticed that Charlie Damker was still wearing the paint-spattered pants he'd had on the night before.

"Well, I dunno . . ."

"Right now!" Dave's eyes blazed, his weight shifted over to his left foot.

"Yes," Damker said. "I'm some sorry about —"

"Don't tell me."

Dave went out the back door, cut across the alley and went into the rear door of Tom Fancher's Furniture and Funeral Parlor.

He found Fancher dressed in a black suit, whistling a tune as he ran a feather duster over the marble top of a small walnut commode. He quit whistling when he saw Dave approaching.

"Lock up," Dave said. "We're goin' out to the bridge."

"I can't . . ." Tom Fancher's protest trailed off as he saw the fury in Cromwell's eyes.

"The hell you can't — move."

The dray was loaded with four long pine boxes when Dave and Tom Fancher climbed aboard.

"The bridge?" old Lou asked, clucking to the team.

"No, swing by the *Record Republican* first. We ought to have an honest, courageous newspaperman along to write the story." Dave had no trace of a smile on his rugged face.

Old Lou turned the team into First Street and stopped in front of the *Record* office. Dave strode purposely across the boardwalk, into the office.

He found Oakley Hunter seated at a large desk, writing on a tablet.

"C'mon, we're goin' out to the bridge."

"I'm busy." Oakley Hunter yawned tiredly.

"Don't make me ornery," Dave came back at him. "You're goin' to come out to the bridge and write about what your work looks like in the daylight."

"You can't bluff me!" Oakley Hunter got to his feet and stood like a banty rooster facing the big rancher.

"I ain't bluffin', you runt of a hog," Dave said, then pushed his thumb up under the chin of the journalist, lifting his face back.

"I'll ruin you, mister," Hunter said huskily, holding his chin with the palm of his soft hand.

"C'mon. Bring your paper and pencil. We're goin'."

"I told 'em not to. You heard me —"

"No, I didn't hear it. C'mon, I said."

Pushing the journalist ahead, Dave boosted him up onto the wagon with Tom Fancher and climbed up beside Lou.

People on the boardwalk stopped to watch the heavy wagon pass by. Shopkeepers came to their open doors with expressions on their faces ranging from sick despair to righteous anger.

Dave caught a glimpse of Eloise Abbott as she peered out a window of the school before ducking away. On the other side of the road, Reverend P. G. Edenfield watched the wagon pass from behind a lace curtain.

In a few minutes they came to the railway trestle and saw the four bodies swinging slowly back and forth, pressed by the mourning prairie wind.

Overhead a pair of vultures descended in a slow circle.

Smoky Hill Cemetery, only a rise of prairie ground overlooking the river, was not even enclosed by a rail fence or organized into spaces.

The wind sighed sadly over the shabby graves with wooden headboards already tilted and falling down. It seemed less like a cemetery than a place to dispose of bodies.

From the elevation, though, Dave could see the hodgepodge town, the wagon trail coming from east and going west, the meandering river and the railroad tracks crossing on the trestle. Looking far off to the north he could see the distant shapes of his barn and cabin which he'd left untended.

*I want to get back there,* he thought. *I want to get clean.*

Si Brown, the town drunk and gravedigger, had the graves already dug as Dave had asked him to do.

"I need a drink," he said.

"Won't be long," Dave said and nodded to Tom Fancher to help unload the boxes.

He made sure the Kentucky boy's coffin was at the west end and that Curly and Frank Rostetter were side by side, gave Si two silver dollars and said, "Fill 'em in, Si."

To Tom Fancher and Charlie Damker he said, "I want you to take care of the headboards. Charge 'em to the city council, and don't be cheap."

Turning to the newspaperman, Oakley Hunter, he said, "Make sure you've got their names right, and you can put in that the boy was born in Hornbeak, Kentucky."

"That all?" Oakley Hunter asked, sweating from the labor and the noonday sun.

"You write in your paper the truth of

how they was murdered. That's all I want."

"Kathy Doran's funeral's going to be to-morrow. You want me to write how she was killed?" Oakley Hunter sneered.

"Just so you say it was an accident that nobody wanted to happen. That's the truth."

"Ain't nobody goin' to say a prayer?" Si Brown asked, wiping his red nose with the back of his hand.

"They had their prayer last night," Dave Cromwell said grimly. "Wherever they was goin', they're already there by now."

Back in town, Dave went into the marshal's office, collected his shotgun and .44-40 off the wall pegs, looked around at the empty rooms still showing signs of the struggle of the night before, then joined Lou Wolford outside at the hitchrail.

"Ready?"

"I packed my spare shirt," the laconic old man said.

They mounted their horses and rode easily up First to River Road, turned left at the schoolhouse, and headed north.

"I was hopin' to learn some readin' and writin' this winter from Miss Eloise."

"Maybe by wintertime the dust will be settled some."

They silently followed the slow-moving

river about two miles before Dave said, "There she is — the Circle C."

"Needs work," Lou Wolford nodded.

Indeed, there was only the small cabin, a larger barn, and a corral built roughly of cottonwood rails. Off near the river grazed a small herd of cattle and a few horses.

"This section is mine, and I'm leasin' two more on north. I'd like to put some young stockers on the grass while it's green."

"I reckon we could pick some out of the Texas herds before they sell to the Ellsworth brokers."

"I just want to get to work," Dave said intensely. "I want to work so hard I can't hear what I hear, or remember what I remember. I want to be so tired I'll never dream again."

As the pair rolled up their sleeves and went to work, the town of Ellsworth was already changing. Not so much as a result of the lynching of the four men, but from the advance of the Santa Fe Railroad west to Dodge City. Cattle pens were being rushed to completion and riders were sent south by cattle brokers to divert some of the herds to the more accessible railhead.

Town life in Ellsworth resumed its usual

pattern after the townsfolk had gotten over the shock of Kathy Doran's death, and the constant wind had softened the mounds of earth on Smoky Hill. Cattle were still coming through from Texas, but their numbers diminished as news of the new Dodge City shipping point spread.

The day after Dave Cromwell had taken off his brass star, Roy Abbott called a council meeting for the purpose of replacing him.

"He's fast with a six-gun, he's big, and he don't back down," Roy Abbott announced to councilmen Oakley Hunter, Wayne Askey, Del Morton, and Phil Meredith.

"Gus Fallon?" Meredith asked skeptically. "He's got nothin'. How does he live?"

"He gambles some," Del Morton said.

"We need an honest man," Oakley Hunter said.

"Everyone knows him," Roy Abbott said.

"I don't know if a gunfighter is what we need," Wayne Askey worried. "Business is already fallin' off."

"It's just temporary," Roy Abbott said. "There's new people coming in every day on the train."

"Maybe it wouldn't hurt to have a strong

man keepin' the peace," Del Morton said. "That cussed Cromwell was such a do-gooder, it was no wonder we had so much trouble."

"Whatever's right," nodded Wayne Askey.

"He's got my vote," Phil Meredith said decisively.

"Then I'll give him the badge," Roy Abbott smiled, "and I might just suggest to him that Cromwell is a threat to the peaceful citizens of Ellsworth."

"Well, I wouldn't antagonize Cromwell overmuch," Oakley Hunter said. "He's stretched out about as tight as he can stand it."

Gus Fallon accepted the badge and the office as calmly as he accepted everything else that came his way. He was a gambler with a practiced nonchalance, his dark, impassive features revealing nothing.

A big man, slightly gone to fat with the years, he had outgunned another gambler in the Red Dog Saloon his first day in town and established that he was a man to be taken seriously.

He had carefully stayed clear of law-breaking, because he was trying to obliterate his checkered past. He'd learned that certain events compound their trouble. If you happen to kill too many innocent strangers one after the other, the emotions grow faster and hotter than they should, and the next thing you know, you're dead or on the run.

His wardrobe was all black, from boots to hat, because he thought it instilled an extra measure of respect in anyone he played cards with.

Putting a badge on that black shirt would draw him out of his anonymity, but it couldn't be helped. Better to trade a little public openness to gain the mantle of a respectable lawman.

Whether from the competition of Dodge City or the lynching, the town's riotous nights cooled off some, making a lot less work. Now Gus Fallon could stroll up the boardwalk in the evening with two six-shooters buckled down on his hips, and you could hear the crickets sing.

As the summer progressed, the grass dried out yellow and the herds had a harder time as water holes dried up and feed grew scarce. This made for the drovers being spookier and raspier than the earlier happy-go-lucky cowboys. A streak of meanness in the newcomers rose as the temperature climbed.

Nonetheless, Ellsworth was growing. The train was bringing in milled lumber and hardware for new buildings to house new businesses. A store that sold only men's clothes opened up and cut into Roy Abbott's general merchandise business. Quickly he added a regular butcher shop that sold beef, fresh or jerked; pork, fresh, salted, or smoked; and eggs, milk, butter, and lard.

A farm implement store and a photography studio opened, as well as a Chinese restaurant that had everyone scared they were eating dog chow mein.

Among these newcomers was a very tall and thin man who seemed at first comical. People called him "the long toothpick," or they said he looked as if he took a bath in a goosegun barrel, and others said he looked half again as high as a bull buffalo.

He wore a shiny, black suit that had been mended here and there by a tidy woman, and a white shirt. He carried a carpet bag to the Hotel Ritz and asked the price of a room. On hearing that, he found his way over to Third Street, where Ma Dove offered room and board at a reasonable price.

"You can come in the back door if you're out late," she said, and sizing him up, added, "I ain't got a bed long enough for you."

"Once when I was a boy I complained so much about having to sleep in a short bed, my daddy offered to cut me off at the knees. 'No, thanks,' I said, 'I reckon they'll learn to bend.'"

"Where you from, Mister . . ." Ma Dove asked with a smile.

"Tyson Tuck, ma'am. I come from Beegum, Tennessee. Do you know that country?"

"No, I never been over the big river," she said. "You be here long?"

"I'm hoping to find a business here if the place is peaceable and shows promise."

"It's been real peaceable since the strangler's jury did their work," Ma Dove declared bitterly. "Those Texas buckaroos are just tiptoein' around like they couldn't lick their upper lip."

"Strangler's jury? I've never heard of it."

"It's supposed to be a secret. Everybody knows who's in it. They say Mick Malone was the worst. He's been drunk down at the Drover's Rest ever since. And not just him. There's plenty more around lookin' like they'd like to puke it up if they could."

"The Drover's Rest . . ."

"That's his'n. What kind a business you lookin' to start, Mr. Tuck?"

Looking down at her as if from a pine

tree, he smiled and said, "I'll have to look around first. A man never knows what might turn up. Maybe the strangler's jury needs a rope maker."

"That's somethin' I wouldn't joke about, Mr. Tuck," Ma Dove said very seriously. "Best say nothin', it might be unhealthy."

"Thank you, ma'am, I'll bear that in mind," he said solemnly.

The rest of the day and evening the tall, gaunt stranger named Tyson Tuck visited the various businesses in town and stopped for a glass of beer in the Red Dog and a glass of whiskey in the Drover's Rest.

Quiet and unassuming, he always chuckled when some drunken cowboy would look up at him and say, "How's the weather up there?"

When it was time to go to supper at Ma Dove's, he arrived right on time.

"What do you think of our town?" she asked as she put a clean plate in front of him.

"Very peaceable. The marshal seems suited to his job, and the Texans respect him."

"That's Gus Fallon. He took over from Dave Cromwell. Cromwell had a bellyful after the stranglers tied him up and hung his prisoners."

"That's natural, I'd say," Tuck nodded. "What happened to him?"

"He's ranchin' over on the Bullfoot. Him and old man Wolford. Was his deputy. Good enough man, but he just wore out."

"It happens to all of us," Tuck said, buttering a biscuit. "I suppose they're lucky the stranglers didn't hang them too."

"They didn't dare hang 'em. You see, about everybody in a small town knows everybody else's business, so everybody knows who is doin' what. That Cromwell is well liked and was doin' a good job. Folks wouldn'ta swallowed him bein' killed."

"I suppose the stranglers are mostly gamblers and riff-raff — that type of people . . ."

"No, not at all!" she hooted. "They're the pillars of the community, you might say. All the way from Roy Abbott down to Mick Malone."

"I declare," murmured Tuck, and helped himself to another piece of fried steak.

"Sure! Oakley Hunter thinks he's such a big mucky muck with his newspaper, and Phil Meredith, the banker, Wayne Askey, and Del Morton — they were all in it."

"I shall sleep the better knowing I'm well protected by such dedicated men," Tuck chuckled.

Finishing his supper, the tall, lean man said goodnight to Ma Dove and retired to the back bedroom.

In the morning, he came into the dining room for breakfast freshly shaven and with a new, clean collar attached to his shirt.

"Good mornin', Mr. Tuck. How is your health and corporosity?" Ma Dove greeted him.

"My health is fine, Mrs. Dove," he chuckled, "but my corporosity is teetolaciously slantindicular."

On the table was a plate of hot muffins covered by a towel, a jar of chokecherry jelly, and butter. When Ma saw him enter, she proceeded to spoon out a bowlful of boiled rolled oats and commenced frying ham and eggs.

He ate hungrily, as if he'd missed supper.

"You do have an appetite," she smiled, putting the platter of ham and eggs before him, and then went back into the kitchen for his coffee.

"It's the quality of the food, ma'am," he said. "I've never tasted better muffins in my life."

"There now, just pile it in," she said happily. "Did you sleep well?"

"Just like a day-old calf with milk on its lips," he nodded. "I didn't hear any gunfire or cowboys yelling. Seems very peaceable."

"I just heard from Mrs. Bartle next door that it wasn't so quiet after all," Ma Dove whispered the gossip, "Mick Malone did the Dutch, he went out sideways."

"I'm sorry, I don't understand."

"Mick Malone up and hung himself."

"How terrible," Tuck said, spearing another muffin with his fork. "Why would he do that?"

"It's no great loss. What he did was tie the rope to a bedstead and then put the noose over his head and jumped out the upstairs window."

"Poor man . . . did he leave any relatives?"

"No, not a soul to mourn him," Ma Dove said sadly.

Tuck finished wiping his plate with the last bite of muffin, took the napkin from his collar, dabbed at his mobile lips, and said, "This may be an opportunity for me."

"How do you mean, Mr. Tuck?"

"I mean I think I'll go into the saloon business." Tyson Tuck smiled. "Back in Tennessee they make pure sippin' whiskey, not this white lightnin' that'd gag a skunk. My brother Percy back there in Beegum makes the best there is."

"You mean you'd take over the Drover's

Rest?" she asked, flabbergasted.

"I'm speakin' without knowing all the facts," Tuck said, "but I have a supply of fine liquor and there is a saloon that could use considerable improvement."

Ma Dove was somewhat puzzled. "Well, I'm not against saloons like some. I expect Phil Meredith owns the building. You'd need to buy the lease from him."

"Then I best talk to him first off."

"Somehow you don't look like a saloonkeeper." She looked up at him questioningly.

"You may be right." He stood tall and smiled down at her. "What do I look like I ought to be?"

"Well . . ." She looked away and laughed. "If I didn't know President Lincoln was dead, I'd think you was him."

"You are a person with rare discernment. Lincoln was a distant relative to us by way of his mother, Mary Hanks, down in Tennessee. I suppose I have his general build, but not nearly his intelligence."

"Well, we can't have everything," she said merrily, and she waddled back into the kitchen while Tuck slipped on his black suit coat and went out the front door.

He found Phil Meredith at his desk in the rear of the brick building where he could watch the teller and clerk and customers without any overt interest.

"Yessir, Mr. Tuck," Phil Meredith said, putting on a flinty smile, "I couldn't help noticing you walking about town yesterday. What can I do for you?"

"I heard the sad news only a few minutes ago, about the owner of the Drover's Rest."

"Yes. Mick Malone jumped," Meredith smiled. "Very sad."

"Who owns the building?"

"I do."

"Then may I buy the lease and bring in some drinkable beverage and clean up the place?"

"Why not, Mr. Tuck, why not?" The banker felt a sudden tremor of fear in his chest and wondered why. He could think of no reason, and decided it was just because the stranger was so goddamned tall.

What had Mick Malone said out there? *Next time hang 'em with a shorter rope . . .*

# 4

Dave Cromwell had bought the big black stud from the trader because he wanted to upgrade his remuda. He had a dozen good brood mares in the remuda, but they were being caught and bred by feral mustangs, range stallions that were more wolf than horse. They were tough fighters, but they were small and rough — with short necks, keg heads, and erect manes — close-coupled, and hard to train.

Dave could foresee a time when the mustang would be replaced by thoroughbreds and Morgans as roads developed and riding became more of a pleasure than a business.

The trader had declared the black sound, but they'd had to choke him down to check his hooves and pasterns, cannon and knees, and hope he wasn't foundered or short-winded, or carrying bots or internal parasites.

The trader had suggested that since he was hardly halter broke and already four years old, he'd best be used solely for breeding, which in horseman's language probably meant that some of the best bronc riders around had tried and failed to ride him.

"He ever killed anybody?" old Lou asked mildly.

"No, but there's always a chance with that strong a horse, he'll throw a rider against the corral or snubbin' post."

As horsetraders go, the man was honest as most, and Dave ended up trading him two saddle-broke geldings, good-enough cow ponies, but nowhere in the class of the black stallion who was seventeen hands tall with a deep chest, powerful hindquarters, a graceful neck, and an Arab head with a broad forehead and an air of pride in the imperious way he surveyed the world.

Dave kept him in a stout corral for a week, disturbing him only at feeding time. He'd fought the corral at first and nicked his chest on the poles, but gradually he settled down as he came to realize this was where he lived.

In the next week, Dave took out extra time to rope him and tie him close to the snubbin' post in the center of the corral, and go over him with a gunny sack, wiping him down and talking to him like he was a friend.

Dave decided to call him Coalie, and the more he worked with him, the more he admired his intelligence and proud spirit.

He didn't want to crush that spirit, nor humble the stallion. Rather, he wanted it to be an alliance between him and the big horse. He felt beholden to no one but himself — why shouldn't his horse feel the same way?

So he took his time, patiently accustoming Coalie to the rope and the sack, the hands and the voice.

If Coalie tried to back off or rear up, to strike with his forelegs, Dave let him fight against the rope, talking to him in a friendly fashion, until he'd settle down again and let his neck be patted and his mane brushed.

After a few days Dave put a halter on him and let him wear it awhile before he snapped a lead rope to it and led Coalie around the corral in perfect docility.

"Now he's really broke to halter," Dave grinned.

"I'd say that was some improvement," old Lou grinned. "He's a smart one."

Day by day Coalie became less tense and less suspicious and would come to the fence for his oats, whinnying a welcome.

Then he permitted a saddle blanket to

be put on his back time after time.

Next, Dave fitted him with a bridle that had a simple bar bit. No longer did Coalie go into a sweat and tremble or try to rear up and fight. It was as if he'd decided to place his confidence in the quiet-talking big cowboy who came to talk to him every day.

The training of Coalie was only a small part of Dave's day, for there was building to be done, cattle to be marked and branded and salted, and moved from one range to another. The mares had to be watched when they were in foal. Hay had to be bought and stacked for winter. When the bills came due, some stock had to be cut out, driven to the railhead, and sold for cash money.

Dave rarely bothered Lou unless it was a job that took two men. He wanted to work himself out of the sickness in his soul that had come with the strangler's jury. He wanted to put that part of his life forever out of his mind, even though it was impossible to do. He could still hear the squeak of the rope and the crack of bones, and sometimes he was awakened from a nightmare by old Lou, who patted him on the shoulder and talked softly, as if gentling a wild horse.

Lou did the cooking and cleaning, and he bought a few hens and a rooster so that they had fresh eggs every day. He did the shopping in town and sometimes rode along with Dave if he was needed.

He brought the news from town that Mick Malone had hanged himself, Gus Fallon was the new marshal, and a newcomer had taken over the Drover's Rest and was trying to make a cleaner, safer place of it.

"That's one less for me to dream about," Dave said.

The overly tall Tyson Tuck seemed to know little about saloons, but he also seemed to know what he wanted. Barrels of aged whiskey arrived by train from Tennessee and were decanted into clean bottles. He hired a Mexican named Luis Javier Fajardo to do nothing but clean and wash everything, from mopping the floor to shining the brass spittoons to washing the bar glasses in soapy water. When he had nothing else to do, Luis Javier washed the walls and shined the hanging brass lamps. The place began to smell more like pine oil than spilled rotgut, and you could see out the windows.

He nailed up a board with pegs on it and the sign Check Guns Here.

The first evening the pegboard appeared, there was a general resentment amongst the customers, but Tuck looked down at them, cleared his throat and bobbed his Adam's apple a couple of times before announcing in an inelegant drawl, "Boys, I ain't servin' anybody wearin' guns."

"You're servin' me," one particularly obnoxious Texan growled, and he went for his gun.

Quick as a cat Tuck had leaped forward and with his long right arm struck downward, catching the gunman on the cheekbone with a large, rocklike fist which not only tore a flap of flesh off the man's face, but dropped him like a coldcocked steer. One of his friends dragged him outside, while the others unbuckled their gunbelts and hung up their hardware.

Luis Javier, the swamper and part-time bartender, also had a guitar and, coming from the border country, could play and sing the cowboy's favorites like "The Old Chisolm Trail," "Stewball," "The Girl I Left Behind Me," and for a change, "El Abandonado."

He was a small, slender man with flashing, merry eyes and a ready smile.

The cowboys gladly pitched their coins into the embroidered sombrero he passed around occasionally.

If someone started hooting and hollering, the others would hush him up, saying "I can't hear the song — dally your tongue, quiet in the peanut gallery!" and such joshing that the mood of the place became more subdued with old-time humor, and those rannies who liked to hoot and holler and fight and shoot drifted over to the Red Dog Saloon across the street.

It happened then that those who wanted a quiet drink went to the Drover's Rest and the others went the other way, and no feelings were hurt.

Gus Fallon checked by occasionally but usually found a clean, pleasant room full of men talking or playing cards or listening to the *cantoro*. He preferred the Red Dog, where there was more action. He had already killed one man in there.

It was this kind of atmosphere that Dave Cromwell and old Lou found when they'd finished selling half a dozen steers to the new butcher in town, a German who had entered into competition with the Mercantile. They'd delivered the beeves to the butcher's corral by the slaughterhouse and rode up First Street to the Drover's Rest. It was the first time Dave had come into town since the night of the lynching.

He looked neither left nor right, but rode with a straight back on his buckskin cow pony with old Lou by his side.

After hanging up their gunbelts, they walked across the fresh wood shavings on the floor that smelled of pine trees and found space at the gleaming bar.

"Your pleasure, friends?" the beanpole Tyson Tuck asked.

"We heard you had some real Tennessee sippin' whiskey," Dave said, looking up into the face of the bartender who somehow seemed familiar. "Do I know you from somewhere? I'm Dave Cromwell. This is Lou Wolford."

"I don't think we've ever met," tall, thin Tuck answered, setting a sparkling bottle and glasses before the pair, then shaking hands. "I'm Ty Tuck from Tennessee," he chuckled.

"Somethin' about your face . . ." Dave stammered, then added, "Don't mind me, Mr. Tuck, I been imaginin' a lot of things lately."

"Folks say good things about you, Dave. Heard you took a beating to save those four unlucky souls and gave 'em a decent burial too."

"It's somethin' I'm tryin' to forget," Dave said.

"I'm right proud to know you." Tuck's eyes bored into Dave's.

"I'm glad I've got one friend in this town," Dave smiled. "Ridin' down the middle of the street, I kept thinkin' there was about a dozen rifles aimed at my backbone."

"I heard Del Morton went off drinkin' at the Red Dog last night but never made it back home . . ." Lou murmured.

"Where do you suppose he could get lost in a small town like this?" Tuck asked.

"They're lookin' along both sides of the river," Lou responded.

"I hardly know the man," Tuck replied from his lofty height, "but he's not exactly impressive."

"He was out there at the bridge that night," Dave mused, "and he could never keep his mouth shut. Likely the stranglers wanted to shut him up."

"I'd reckon they'd try to shut you up first," Tuck surmised softly, watching the doorway.

Carl Doran's cadaverous features were distorted — grey grooves under his eyes made his eyes seem to bulge out all the more wildly.

"Cromwell!" he yelled, awkwardly pulling a Navy Colt .36 from his waistband. "You're doing this!"

With a sweep of his long left arm, Tuck shoved the unarmed Dave aside while with his right hand he threw the bottle.

Carl Doran ducked, lifted the gun, and tried to sight in the rolling Dave.

Tuck dropped behind the bar, came up with a single-barrel sawed-off twelve-gauge and pulled the trigger, sending a dozen heavy buckshot into Doran's body. Doran fired then, trying to kill Dave with his last breath, but the bullet only peeled a groove in the oiled spruce floor padded with fresh sawdust.

It started and ended in the span of less than twenty seconds. Already Luis Javier was arriving with a blanket to cover the body.

"My Lord, you're fast!" Dave said to Tuck as he got to his feet. "Thank you for savin' my life."

"He left me no other course," Tuck said, downcast. "I'm plumb against killing a fellow man unless it's got to be done."

"I don't know what he wanted," Dave said, puzzled. "He said I was doin' this. Doin' what?"

"I reckon it has to do with Mick Malone

and Del Morton," Lou said thoughtfully. "He figured you was pickin' them off one at a time."

"That's understandable," said Tuck, bobbing his head. "You know them all."

"I never saw their faces, but I recognized them easy enough." Dave thought back on it and remembered.

*May you all fry in hell. . . .*

"So he figured you were on to him," Tuck said.

"But I haven't left the ranch in six weeks."

"I suppose you can prove that?" came the voice of Gus Fallon, who lifted the blanket and looked at the bloody corpse of Carl Doran.

"I can vouch for it," Lou Wolford said and put a restraining hand on Dave's arm. "I know you haven't seen him."

"I never seen him —" Gus Fallon turned to face Dave Cromwell, "but I've heard too much already. You think you can make trouble in my town, I'll cut you down to size."

"You want to start right now?" Dave responded quickly.

"I don't fight unarmed men," Gus Fallon replied, "but you get mixed up in any more killin' in this town, I'll come after you whether you're carryin' iron or not."

"Just do your job, Marshal. Start off with arrestin' Roy Abbott, then the banker, the newspaperman, the barber, the same ones that hired you," Dave came back hotly. "I'm out of it."

"You haven't a shred of evidence against them."

"One of them will talk, if you go after him hard enough. You got nine left to pick from."

"Then why didn't you do it when you had the chance? Scared?" Gus Fallon sneered.

"I didn't have the chance," Dave said, knowing that even if he'd had a chance, innocent wives and children of the guilty ones would be punished as badly as the men, especially Eloise Abbott, who somehow had become a person needing his protection.

"It'll blow over soon enough," Tuck said to calm the waters. "But your quarrel should be with me, Marshal. It was me that killed that man."

"He still has the gun in his hand and he fired it in your place," the marshal said. "I've got no quarrel with that."

His blocky, black-clad figure filled the door as he went out.

In a short while, melancholy Tom Fancher arrived with a stretcher and a couple of helpers. His face turned the color of lard as he glanced fearfully at Dave.

"Look, Davy —" he stammered, "you don't have no grudge against me. I did everything you told me to."

"How much did you charge the city council?" Dave asked.

"A nominal sum — covered my expenses . . ." Tom Fancher said nervously. "What I'm saying is, I don't want no trouble with you."

"You haven't anything to worry about me. If I was you, I'd be worryin' about the stranglers tryin' to protect themselves." Dave smiled.

"Those type of people you're talking about, I hear by the gossip, they're armed and very damned dangerous," Tom Fancher protested. "That's all I know. I was home in bed that night."

" 'Here he comes,' " Dave quoted from memory. " 'Let's get it over and done with.' "

Fancher's lardy face turned a pale shade of blue-green, and involuntarily he put his hands over his ears.

"I didn't do nothing more than the rest of them!" he cried out and ran stumbling out the open door, almost knocking down a man wearing ordinary cattleman's clothes and a new stockman's flat-crowned hat.

"He thinks, because everybody else was in it, it makes it right," old Lou ruminated, lighting his pipe, his lined features without expression.

The man in the stockman's hat smiled and ordered a whiskey, when Tuck greeted him with a deadpan, "Welcome to Ellsworth. Peaceful and prosperous."

Tom Fancher spread the news that Carl Doran was dead, and the women friends gathered around the wife who had been left alone in the world.

At the same time, Roy Abbott sent word to eight other members of the committee to meet in the back room of the Drover's Rest.

Putting aside his apron, he picked up Oakley Hunter and Phil Meredith on the way, and going inside the saloon, Roy Abbott asked Tuck perfunctorily for the use of the room where sometimes high-stakes card games were played in private.

"Of course, sir," Tuck said and led them through the door.

"There'll be some others coming," Phil Meredith said. "Leave the door open."

"Yessir."

"And bring us a bottle of your best Tennessee sour mash and some glasses," Oakley Hunter ordered.

"Right away, sir."

"Nice fellow," commented Oakley Hunter.

"Smart businessman," Phil Meredith said.

"I don't trust him," Roy Abbott said, "but then, I don't trust anyone anymore."

In a few minutes the others of the committee had crowded around the large table covered with green baize and helped themselves to the bottle.

"Close the door, Charlie," Roy Abbott said. "We're all here but Edenfield, and we don't want him anyways."

Seeing that the door was closed, he continued, "Carl was killed today because he figured out that Dave Cromwell is set on revenge. Carl walked right into a trap, and now we've lost three of our committee."

"But Mick Malone committed suicide —" said George Philbrick, the barber, laughing nervously and rolling his eyes.

"I don't think so. Not anymore. We're being killed," Roy Abbott said, "and somehow Cromwell's behind it."

"How can we be sure?" Tom Fancher asked.

"It's his way of getting back at us," Phil Meredith said. "We humbled his pride and now he thinks he can murder us all in cold blood."

"But couldn't it be somebody else?" Bert Gwinner objected. "Curly and Frank had a lot of friends in the cattle camps."

"All right, it's a possibility, but we don't know any of them, and we do know that Dave Cromwell made a threat against all of us."

"I'm a witness to that," Phil Meredith said.

"What have you got in mind?" Wayne Askey asked, his pinched face drawn tight over his cheekbones and his fingers drumming on the table.

"Somebody has to go out to his ranch and shoot him."

"There's none of us as fast as him," Oakley Hunter protested into the dead silence.

"But any one of us can hit a target at three hundred yards," Roy Abbott said.

"Ambush," Bert Gwinner said. "I like it."

"I never thought I'd ever be a bushwhacker," Phil Meredith said. "I doubt I can do it."

"If you can't, you can pay somebody to take your place," Roy Abbott said decisively. "Cut the cards. High card wins the job."

Roy Abbott spread the deck out like a fan. "Start with Oakley."

Oakley Hunter fetched out a card and turned over a ten of hearts. Wayne Askey drew a trey of clubs, George Philbrick drew a ten of spades, Bert Gwinner slipped out a seven of hearts, Tom Fancher drew a queen of clubs and cursed, Roy Abbott flipped over a king of diamonds and said, "Good. I want the job."

Phil Meredith said, "Wait — you left me out," and turned over the ace of spades.

"Wouldn't you know it," he said. "I can't shoot anything."

"I'll do it for five hundred dollars," Bert Gwinner grinned, showing his yellow, broken teeth.

"No other offers?" Meredith looked around at the group. "All right, Bert, it's a deal."

"You have a good rifle?" Roy Abbott asked.

"I'm used to my Springfield .45-70." Gwinner grinned. "It'll take out a buffalo."

"Do it soon." Roy Abbott looked over his shoulder nervously. "Meetin's adjourned, and no one speaks of this ever again. Understood?"

"Understood," the men agreed and, finishing the bottle, rose and drifted out single file to the street.

No one said a word of farewell or thanks to Tuck, nor did anyone bother to look around the barroom as they passed through.

"Proud bunch," the man in the cream-colored ranchman's hat said to Tuck after they'd gone.

"They appear to have weighty things on their minds," Tuck smiled.

"Mind if I play some solitaire?" the stranger asked. "I'm goin' to be waitin' around awhile."

"Not at all, stranger. Help yourself." Tuck nodded agreeably.

Riding up First Street, Dave and Lou turned left on River Road as usual and, passing the school, Dave saw Eloise Abbott and the marshal standing on the front porch, talking.

Standing close together, they seemed unaware of Dave and Lou passing by. Gus Fallon was holding her hand, and she showed no sign of resisting.

What had come over that girl?

"Steady on, son," old Lou said. "We got a ways to go yet."

"I've got my guns now," Dave said.

"They say he's fast as a cut cat."

"Then maybe I'm a better shot!" Dave retorted angrily.

"We got a ranch with cows and horses, especially that good Coalie, to worry about," Lou said to give his young friend something to think about.

"I reckon." Dave glumly settled down to ride along the river.

After turning out his buckskin to roll and drink, the first thing Dave did was to go over to Coalie's corral with a bucket of oats.

The big black whinnied a welcome and arched his shining neck.

"Much horse," Lou commented.

"Think he's about ready to ride?"

"For you, yes, for anybody else, I don't think it could be done."

"He's used to carryin' the saddle, lungin' around the snubbin' post," Dave said, climbing through the rails and patting the horse's powerful neck.

"He's sure come along fast. That Arab blood in him makes him smart," Lou nodded. "He's already worth twenty of them cayuses we're workin'."

"I don't care what he's worth, I sure as hell won't sell him."

Dave let Coalie eat from the bucket

while he walked around the big horse, his hands always on the supple skin, his voice always softly talking nonsense understandable to a smart horse.

"So now, big boy, we're just takin' a little *pasear* aroundabouty, and if you want to cave in my ribs, I reckon right about now would be a good time to try it. . . ."

But the stud never cocked his hoof as Dave made the tour around him, coming back to the wide head.

The black horse looked at him agreeably, grinding up the oats between his back teeth.

"I'm goin' to do it," Dave decided suddenly.

Walking to the rail, he shook out his dry saddle blanket and laid it carefully over Coalie's back, taking a lot of time smoothing it out and making little adjustments. Next he went to the rail for his saddle, securing the stirrups and cinch to the horn so as to not have anything flopping around, placed the saddle carefully just behind the withers, and eased the stirrups and double cinch down. Coalie stamped his foot, but stood without his bridle.

Dave took up on the cinches, then went back to the railing for the bridle and slipped it over the handsome head without hurting the alert ears. Laying the reins back on Coalie's neck, he went back to the saddle and tightened the cinches again. Then, taking a deep breath, he held the reins in his left hand, put his left boot in the stirrup, and facing the rear where he could see a kick or a buck coming, he made his normal mounting and had his right boot in the stirrup before Coalie knew that he had a rider on his back.

Instead of jamming in the spurs and hanging on to the saddle horn, Dave said, "Good boy," and swung his right leg back over, pivoting on his left, and dismounted. Then he led Coalie around the corral once and mounted him again with the same easy motion.

After repeating this lesson four times and talking quietly all the while, he mounted again, lifted the reins, leaned a hair forward, and tightened his knees a fraction. Coalie commenced walking around the corral as easy as apple pie.

Dave could hardly keep from shouting out his joy at finding such a fine animal, but he kept a poker face and controlled his voice.

Lou Wolford looked on with an impassive face but with a certain gladness in his heart. Dave needed such an animal badly, needed a strong friend that matched him well, and here that friend was.

Dave let the reins slack instead of pulling on them, and Coalie stopped instantly.

"Perfect, Coalie. I bet you're some smarter'n me." Dave smiled, dismounted, and unsaddled the big black, who looked to be disappointed that he hadn't gotten to even trot yet.

"Tomorrow we'll go out, I promise, Coalie," Dave said, and he rubbed him down with the gunny sack whether he needed it or not.

Two days later Lou Wolford went to town for fresh supplies and returned in the afternoon with the news that Del Morton's body had been found.

Dave's mind flashed on a remembrance he wanted to forget.

*Why don't we take down their pants and see what they got first?*

"It was downriver about a mile, snagged on some downed cottonwoods."

"Probably fell in drunk and drowned."

"He didn't drown. Somebody put a piece of baling wire around his neck and took a quick turn on it. It must've been quicker'n an alligator can chew a pup."

"Town upset?"

"Things are mighty quiet around the Mercantile and the bank and barber shop. But they won't take it lyin' down."

"Dry gulchin'?"

Lou nodded. "I just doubt if they trust each other enough to come out in one bunch and fight it straight up and down."

"Maybe you oughta take a trip down to see your kids in Texas."

"Hell, Dave, I ain't even married," Lou said with painful shock. "And I ain't goin' to be tolled away from a fight."

"Anybody layin' out there in the trees by the river could pick us off when we come out in the morning," Dave murmured. "Let's take a ride."

Saddling up Coalie, he put the big horse in an easy lope with Lou on his bay at his side. Coming to three hundred yards from the cabin, Dave started a slow circle, looking for a likely place for a bush-whacker to hide.

The prairie was wide open and flat, without a rock or ravine to hide a rifleman. Continuing the circle, he came to a point on the Bullfoot where the riverbank had slid down, providing a perfect place to hide a horse and rifleman.

"That'll do it," commented Lou as they dismounted.

Dave kneeled and sighted in the cabin door with his short rifle.

"I say we flip a coin as to who goes out first in the mornin'," Dave chuckled. "I do wish that door faced west now."

"Want me to set out here tonight?" Lou asked. "I can get the drop on him before he ever gets settled."

"I reckon not." Dave shook his head. "I'd as liefer climb out the back window in the mornin' as have you settin' out here battin' mosquitoes and kickin' out rattlesnakes all night."

"I swear . . ." The old man shook his head sadly, as if Dave had lost his mind.

"Fact is, Lou, we're goin' to move our goods to the barn and do some scouting just before daybreak. That suit you?"

"I figured we ought to discourage whatever varmints are plannin' to take our scalps."

After a simple supper, they carried their bedrolls and other gear to the barn and made their beds in the loft on some loose hay. Each had his sidearms and rifle alongside him when they bedded down.

Bert Gwinner had been born on a farm in Ohio. The Gwinner family might have been well off except that Bert's father wanted more and more sons to help work the land and increase the size of the farm. As each son grew old enough to think for himself, he had only to look at the hard, disciplined slavery imposed by his ambitious father before heading off west to the goldfields. He would have been a loonie to choose the farm.

As Bert Gwinner came to the age of fourteen, he had five brothers and sisters who had already left home, five little ones behind him, and his mother was dying.

When he was fifteen, he stole his father's best horse and rode as hard as he could toward Springfield, Illinois, where he thought he could hook up with a wagon train going to California.

He was still a gangly boy who hadn't reached his full size yet, and as such was at the bottom of the abundant labor market.

It hadn't been easy, he reflected, as he rode a ribby chestnut gelding along the river in the moonlight.

Lots of times he'd been glad to eat scraps thrown out by strangers, and other times he'd eaten corn filched from farmers' wagons, but he'd made it through on his own and was proud of himself.

Drifting along through California, he

found work on the big cattle ranches, but he didn't like the easygoing Mexicans because he couldn't understand their language, and he was always afraid they'd cut his throat some night. Still, he'd had some fun with the señoritas, living with one for several months until she became pregnant and it was time for him to hit the trail again.

She was pretty enough, he reflected, but they aged quickly.

No, he'd done the right thing, getting out while there was still time.

There'd still been some hard times, especially coming through the Apache country, but once he'd reached Santa Fe, things turned for the better. He'd worked for an old drayman there, driving a wagon pulled by six mules between Santa Fe and Lordsburg, and then one day he found the old man dead.

He'd taken the team and wagon, tied four horses to the tailgate, and drove east toward Kansas to start a livery business.

He'd never killed a man in his life, he thought, but poor folks have poor ways, and five hundred dollars was a fortune for one night's work.

Besides, he had a special hatred for Dave Cromwell for the uppity way he treated him bringing back the bodies. *No man tells Bert Gwinner what to do. This man has seen the elephant and rode the trails, and he ain't just about to get down on his knees and kiss Mr. Dave Cromwell's boots.* So, deep in thought, remembering the old days, he failed to hear the soft hoofbeats of a rider following him in the shadows.

As he dismounted in the woods across the pasture from the ranch house, he thought about buying another wagon and some good mules and start hauling freight between Lincoln and Ellsworth. It would double his business. *Increase — that's what I want, and that's what I'm going to get.*

Hiding the chestnut and hunkering down in his covert, he thought he could sleep a couple hours before sunrise.

They slept lightly through the night, and just before daylight, Dave put on his hat and boots and whispered to Lou. "You cover me."

Lou thought about it for a moment and nodded. "That's best."

With his Colt .45 and short rifle, Dave made his way behind the cover of the water trough and chicken coop, the scanty protection of the rail fence, then, pausing to scan the dark trees by the river, he suddenly darted to the left and threw himself behind a tumbleweed.

There was no shot — nothing.

Crawling on his belly with the rifle ahead of him, he'd gained the shelter of a fallen log and crept to the right.

Here there was little light and strange shadows. Heart pounding, he worked around a thicket of chokecherries, then rolled over a log and crept to the place he and Lou had spotted the afternoon before. There was no movement on the shelf, and then in the shadows behind a tree he saw the outline of a standing chestnut horse. Waiting longer for a tad more light, he held back from charging the ambuscade, then he saw the shine of a spur rowel glinting, and from the deep shadow he picked out the figure of a man lying at an odd angle.

"Up!" he called, the rifle holding dead center on the figure.

There was no movement, no sound.

"I said get your hands up!" he said loudly, ready to fire, but there was nothing except the faint whicker of the horse.

Stepping carefully forward, he set the rifle muzzle on the back of the man and then reached down to take the long rifle from underneath him.

The hand was cold, rigid.

Backing away, he thought grimly that someone had done his work for him and that there would surely be hell to pay for it.

Stepping out into the open, he waved at the barn and waited until Lou bowlegged across the flatland to his side.

"There's a dead man in there," Dave said quietly. "I figured better we look at him together."

"Shot?"

"I dunno —" said Dave, leading the way back into the timber.

By now the sun was on the rise and daylight filtered into the trees. The man was dressed in dungarees and chambray shirt. There was no wound in his back, and when they rolled Bert Gwinner there was no wound on the front either.

Eyes bulging in terror and mouth open, exposing yellow teeth, Bert Gwinner had died of strangulation.

"It's a wire," Dave said, pointing to the twist on the back of Gwinner's neck.

"Don't make much difference," Lou Wolford said, "he's sure deader'n hell."

*Hang the sonsabitches!*

"That's four down," Dave said.

# 5

Dave and Lou came down River Road past the school and turned right on First Street, where the Drover's Rest anchored the corner, and slowly proceeded down the middle of the street. Dave rode Coalie for the first time off the ranch. Lou sat astride his bay, and dallied to his saddle horn was a lead rope secured to Gwinner's chestnut, plodding along behind with its grisly burden tied to the saddle.

Gwinner had been a big man and made a big corpse. His boots on the near side nearly touched the ground and his swaying hands on the offside appeared to be reaching for the dust in the street.

Dave was glad the school hadn't let out for dinner yet. He hadn't taken time to wrap the body in a blanket. He hadn't taken time for anything. All he wanted was to get the carcass off the ranch and bring it back to where it came from.

Henry Darby, a sometime swamper at the Red Dog, saw them at the corner and ran down the boardwalk yelling, "Here they come! They got Bert Gwinner!" as if he were Paul Revere spreading news of vital importance.

Neither Lou or Dave paid him any attention.

The storekeepers peered out their doors fearfully because they knew their scheme had backfired.

Tall Tuck came out of the Drover's Rest and gave a laconic "Howdy," as they passed.

He was joined by the older cattleman in the flat-crowned hat, who was lighting his pipe and taking in the scene.

George Philbrick was shaving Phil Meredith, when he saw Dave and Lou through the window. "Look!" he said, dropping the razor in horror.

Phil Meredith straightened up in the barber chair, and seeing the body of Bert Gwinner draped over the saddle, he cursed, "Goddamn the luck!"

Strangers in the Ritz Hotel stepped out of the lobby to silently watch the grisly procession pass on by while Ed Rowan of the Red Dog Saloon came out with a white towel wrapped around his waist. Recognizing the chestnut, he congratulated himself for protesting against the necktie party and staying clear of it. For sure they'd discouraged the drovers from coming into town for a few drinks and some foolishness. He was thinking of selling out and moving on west to Dodge.

Standing in the front door of the Mercantile, Roy Abbott set his heavy jaw and wiped his hands on his apron. He was thinking that if Bert Gwinner couldn't do it, none of the rest could. They'd need to bring in someone really first class with the gun; someone who would kill for a price. Gus Fallon might be baited into a fight with Cromwell, but he was a wise gunfighter who looked out for his own skin first. Could he arrest Cromwell right this minute for murder? Once in jail, they could hang him like the others. Yet there was something about the body of Bert Gwinner — what was it? No blood. He'd not been shot! What the hell was going on!

Deliberately Abbott stepped out into the street and walked beside the chestnut until he saw the ends of the baling wire twisted at the back of the swollen neck.

Coming to the hitchrail at the jail, Dave Cromwell checked the big, gleaming black and dismounted. He took the lead line from Lou, who had his big two-bore cradled over the pommel of his saddle. Unobtrusively his bay moved sidewise, getting clear of the action, yet ready to control it.

"What the hell!" Gus Fallon came striding out of the marshal's office and went immediately to Gwinner's body. The twisted wire was obvious.

"More of your work?" he glared at Dave.

"We found him by the river just like this. His big rifle was underneath him like he was set to bushwhack us come daybreak," Dave said. "I found five hundred dollars in new golden eagles in his pocket that I'm keepin' until a legal heir turns up."

"Five hundred dollars? Where . . . ?" Gus Fallon growled.

"Yes, where did it come from? Someone in this town paid him to do his dirty work, that's where the money came from. My guess is it come from the bank right there."

"Ridiculous!" Phil Meredith came up, half his face still lathered. "I have nothing at all to do with this."

"I wonder if he gave you a receipt," Dave Cromwell smiled.

"Listen, you worthless saddlebum, you can't talk like that to me!"

"Who did this?" Roy Abbott interrupted, before the paunchy banker made a mistake and said the wrong thing.

"Cromwell's the only one who had any reason," Oakley Hunter said, coming from across the street.

"What reason would that be, other than saving my own life?"

"You're the only one, except old Wolford, who was out there that night . . ."

"You're reachin' too far," Dave said easily. "If I was to want to kill a den of snakes, I'd use a keg of blackpowder, I wouldn't be takin' you out one at a time."

"You're the only one involved."

"Everyone's involved. One of the stranglers is killin' the rest for some reason. Probably his conscience. If I was you and my neck was getting tired from lookin' over my shoulder, I'd talk to the preacher. He ought to have a conscience."

"Couldn't be that baby-faced softy," Wayne Askey said, joining the group.

"Arrest Cromwell!" Roy Abbott said harshly.

"Suppose Gus Fallon here had a notion he could own the whole town if he played his cards right?" Dave said softly. "It's one of you, for sure."

"Watch yourself, Cromwell." Gus Fallon stepped quickly clear and faced Dave. "I'm taking you in for murdering Bert Gwinner."

"Mister, you ain't trappin' me in that jail."

"I'm taking you in."

"I'll go if there's a couple U.S. Marshals

to protect me from these yellow-gutted skunks," Dave said bitterly, his hand hovering over the walnut butt of his Colt.

"Hold it, boys," old Lou said quietly from his saddle. "I reckon if there's any gunplay, I'm goin' to get in it."

Roy Abbott turned angrily toward Lou Wolford and stared into the huge ten-gauge barrels that looked big as railway tunnels.

"I got her loaded with double-ought buck and bent horseshoe nails," Lou said mildly.

Roy Abbott backed away until he tripped on the boardwalk and fell back into the dirt of the street.

"I'm sayin' you better be watchin' each other," Dave Cromwell said, moving to big Coalie. "One of you is playing the exterminator. You'll all be dead in a week if you don't smoke him out."

Wheeling the big horse, Dave smiled down at the pallid faces and added with a smile, "Good luck."

They rode back up the street, tied their horses before the Drover's Rest, and went inside.

Tyson Tuck was placing platters of bread and cheese and sliced roast beef and boiled eggs on the bar as they entered.

"Help yourself, boys," he said, adding a bowl of mustard and another of sliced onions.

Tuck poured them mugs of beer while they built up sandwiches.

Dave glanced at the cattleman in the flat-crowned hat coming up behind them for the free lunch.

"Mighty fine belly-packin' material," Dave nodded to the man.

"Name's Hardisty, Alvin Hardisty," the cattleman said.

"Dave Cromwell and Lou Wolford."

"Looks like you had a hard morning," Hardisty observed, making up a sandwich.

"It ain't our usual way," Lou said. "Ordinarily we like to get up about noon and listen to the rapture of the birds singin', then have some fried chicken and smoke a couple cigars."

"Spoken like a true cattleman," Hardisty smiled. "If it has anything to do with danger or dirt, they crawl back into bed."

"How are things going?" Tuck asked from his lofty height.

"I believe we're losin' more enemies than we're makin'," Dave said and munched on his thick sandwich.

"Who you reckon is behind all this?" Hardisty asked, adding a dollop of mustard and a sliced pickle atop the roast beef.

"Hell, could be anyone except me," Dave said. "Could be you or Tuck or Tom Fancher or Fallon, or somebody out there we don't even know."

"I'm picking the banker, Phil Meredith," Tuck said. "He's got a reason."

"What's that?" Hardisty asked.

"He holds the mortgages, so every time one of our brave citizens dies, he can foreclose."

"Somethin' to that," Lou nodded agreeably. "He'll end up with the drayage and livery business, lock, stock, and barrel."

"It's an idea, but he don't look like he's savvy enough to do it."

"Might be he hires it done. Bankers generally like somebody else to do the dirty work."

"You could just as well say Tom Fancher's doin' it so as to make more funerals, or Charlie Damker in order to sell more coffins," Dave said. "No, I think it's somebody with a conscience. Like he's got some gristle stuck in his craw, he can't swallow until he's killed all his partners."

"None of it makes sense," Hardisty said. "I'm not settling down here until it works itself out, that's for sure."

"Figurin' on ranchin'?" Lou asked.

"The grass is good," Hardisty nodded, "and the land is cheap. It's only the people that make the problems."

"Still, we need some people to eat the beef," Lou said judiciously, brushing crumbs off his shirt front.

"Speakin' of beef," Dave said to Lou, finishing his beer, "maybe we ought to start looking after ours instead of all the troubles in Ellsworth."

"Take care," Tuck said as they went out the door.

Mounting up, they made the turn and came abreast of the school. Dave wanted to stop and ask for Eloise, but he felt it would be too big an imposition just now. He dearly wanted to know if she was speaking to him or whether she was listening to the poison her father had spread about him.

Surely she wouldn't make any commitment to Gus Fallon. Anyone could see he was more outlaw than lawman, a person of low repute and with no thought of family or future on his mind. Yet women were strange, they never made sense and could be stubborn as a switchtail mule. They could drive a thinking man crazy.

Yet he'd thought Eloise might be different. He thought she had a halfway level head, enjoyed teaching the little tykers, and not spending her time with ribbons and beau catchers.

She could ride as well as any cowgirl and seemed to like the country. She'd said, too, she'd be pleased to teach him, come fall. He wondered if she'd changed her mind. For sure, if she thought he was trying to kill her daddy, she'd treat him worse'n a polecat at a picnic.

Keeping his eyes straight ahead, he didn't see her come out of the schoolhouse and hurry across the yard. Not until he heard her call, "Dave!" did he dare look her way and check big Coalie.

Turning in the saddle, he touched his hat brim as she came up close. Lou sort of drifted on as if he had better things to do.

"Ma'am."

"Dave, what's going on?" she asked, out of breath.

"We just brought in Bert Gwinner. He was settin' to dry gulch us until somebody pulled his picket pin."

"Bert Gwinner? Why would he do such a thing?"

"Somebody paid him and somebody else killed him."

"But why?"

"Eloise," he said, stepping down from

the saddle and looking into her dark blue eyes, "it has to do with the strangler's committee. I don't know just how, but it can't be anything else."

"What are you trying to tell me?"

"Your daddy is the he-boar of that committee. He's up to his neck in quicksand."

"Daddy? Nonsense! How can you speak of him that way?"

"Eloise, I'm just tryin' to warn you of somethin' bad up ahead."

Her face flushed with anger. "Maybe he's right. At least Gus Fallon doesn't go around talking behind people's backs."

"Eloise, everybody in town knows about this except you," Dave spoke patiently. "Don't be stubborn or you're goin' to get hurt."

"Stubborn? Is that some sort of a threat, Mr. Cromwell? Well, let me tell you something —"

Before she could get set to let loose both barrels, Dave hung his head, raised both hands, and silently mounted Coalie.

"Wait just a minute . . ." she said angrily, but he merely touched his forefinger to his hat and squeezed his knees slightly, sending Coalie into an easy lope in which he showed his fancy way of going best.

She stood in the road, hands on hips, sputtering until Dave went around the bend and joined up with Lou.

Wayne Askey wasn't one to stand around and wait for orders. Once he'd seen Dave and Lou enter the Drover's Rest, he told his boy to mount up and they rode out the other end of town, then hooked around over open country until they came to the road that led to the Circle C Ranch.

He'd come into the young country when the Comanches had been thick and in a killing mood and knew it better than most. Twice he'd been involved in small running battles with them after they'd raided some over-greedy settler's home, murdered and scalped the unlucky people, and run off with the horses. In one of these battles, he'd killed a big buck and cut off his ears.

Now the Comanches were just about cleared out, the buffalo were gone, and the smallpox was doing its dreadful work among the other hostiles.

With his fourteen-year-old son on a hammerheaded mustang, he rode at a fast trot, saving his horse for later on. As they rode, he thought over his plan. No one would expect a man and a boy to hit back so soon. He'd taken no chances telling anyone what he intended doing because he no longer knew who he could trust. He could trust himself, though, and the job had to be done or they would all be executed one at a time. The time to strike was when they least expected it — like right now, because there wouldn't be anyone watching the ranch or even the range.

His pinched, pockmarked face had a feral quality to it, and when he smiled, his thin teeth protruded like a bloodsucking weasel's.

"Where we goin', Pa?" the boy asked.

"Never mind."

The boy was dressed in patched overalls and brogans and had spent most of his life out on a scrubby ranch in the flint hills where Wayne Askey had settled his wife and family a few years before. The boy was the eldest and did a man's work helping his ma hold the place together while Wayne Askey made the cash money from making and mending harness. Not that much of the money found its way out to the Askeys' Bullseye Ranch. There were always the temptations of the flesh in Ellsworth.

Nonetheless, he'd managed to buy a few scrubby cattle, brand a few mavericks, and register his Bullseye brand.

He'd been thinking lately about that

brand. How you could make a Bullseye out of a Circle C just about as easy as making a running iron out of a cinch ring.

The more he thought over his plan the better he liked it. Depended a little on how long Cromwell waited around town, but if it worked out right, he'd not pay any attention to the missing cattle, he'd just be so mad he'd run back into town and get himself killed.

Wayne Askey had been born in Wisconsin under cloudy circumstances. The Shakers in Peacetown, Wisconsin, had told him he was an orphan, but then, snooping through the record books, he found the notation: "Foundling on doorstep, with note. Name, Wayne Askey. No persons named Askey in County."

That was all he had for a heritage, a name that wasn't even real. Likely there was a Wayne Askey passing through and got a girl in trouble and just kept on going, so he'd ended up as an orphan foundling on a meeting house doorstep.

They'd raised him up strict and taught him all manner of leatherwork, but he couldn't control the urge to peek into the separate women's house or handle their private clothing, eventually succumbing to the sin of forcing a younger girl in the hayloft.

The men had gathered in the meeting house and heard the testimony. Then they'd tied him to a tree, whipped him ten times with a braided blacksnake whip, and then sent him down the road with a small packful of his meager belongings.

He never thought of going back, but rather had gotten work helping a harness maker in Peoria, Illinois. He'd stayed there a year until he raped another girl and was caught. They'd sent him to jail for five years, but he'd escaped with a murderer named Amos Bender and made his way to the frontier after Bender was killed robbing a bank in Jefferson City, Missouri.

He'd had some luck there because he'd held the money bag, riding down the alley with Bender making covering fire. From that one bank robbery he'd learned he never wanted to try it again. He had headed west to the Kansas frontier where he discovered the availability of sporting girls.

No longer need he find a girl weaker than himself and put a knife to her throat to have his way with her. You just put a silver dollar in a sweaty hand and go at it.

Of course, it wasn't near the pleasure of touching fresh young breasts and supple thighs and looking down into the terror-stricken eyes, feeling her give way for him.

But with sporting girls they didn't send you to prison.

Still he had the hog lust fill up in him at times and he would drift down the dark alley behind Roy Abbott's house, hoping to see Eloise through the back window preparing for bed.

Some day, some day, he dreamed he'd catch her out riding by herself, and put the knife to her throat.

"Where we goin', Pa?"

The boy's voice snapped him out of his warm dream and he looked around at the boy hatefully. "Shut your mouth!"

Why he'd ever married that boy's mother was still a mystery to him. He'd come across the ranch laid out on marginal land where the eldest daughter of the owner welcomed him in. He helped the old man around the ranch awhile because the daughter had worked out a way to come over to the barn where he slept, and pretty soon she was pregnant with the boy.

A traveling parson had married them, and not long after, the old man tore his hand shoeing a horse. The laceration didn't seem all that bad, and the old man had spit some tobacco ambeer on it and finished nailing on the shoe.

In ten days he was dead of blood poisoning.

After that, Wayne Askey rustled stray bunches of cattle until Ellsworth made a start and he saw there was a need for a harness maker.

Maybe once a month he got out to the Bullseye Ranch, where he had eight children.

Coming around the bend he saw the cabin and the barn off to the left. A half a mile farther, hidden by a low hill, would be the cattle.

"Hello the house!" he called and waited, making sure no one was about.

"All right, boy," he said, handing his son a box of phosphors. "Go fire the barn. I'll take the cabin."

"Fire the barn?" The boy was caught by surprise.

"Burn it down, damn it, then help me with them steers." Askey swung at the boy and missed as the boy whirled his pony and rode toward the barn.

Askey unfolded a sheet of paper already prepared and put the paper on top of a gatepost held down by a good-sized rock.

Then, leaving his sorrel tied to the post, he went in the unlocked door of the cabin, found a hay-stuffed tick on one of the

118

bunks, ripped it open with his knife, and struck a phosphor. He didn't notice that the bedrolls and warbags were gone. He just lighted the hay, turned, and scurried outside. A single-board-walled cabin, it would burn like pitch pine in minutes.

Mounting up, he rode at a gallop up the hill, yelling at the boy to hurry. Topping the hill, he saw a herd of a hundred beeves feeding on the bottom land.

Inexperienced in barn burning, the boy dropped the phosphor before it could burn his fingers, thinking it fell into the hay manger, when in fact it fell through a slat and landed in an empty tin bucket, where the flame died harmlessly.

By then he was driving the pony away, afraid of what he'd done and afraid of the punishment.

"Up the draw to the creek!" his father yelled at him, waving him off to the left blank of the small herd. "Move 'em out."

*This is worse than barn burning*, the boy thought. *They hang people for this.* Then he was whistling and whipping the critters to get them started up the draw.

The beeves took off on a run, but not a wild stampede. In the draw they were confined, and the two riders could handle them.

119

The draw entered a wide stream that flowed over limestone bedrock, and Askey herded the beeves upstream, keeping them on the rock so they left no tracks.

He knew the country well and had once thought of taking up this ranch before young Cromwell had arrived. The trouble was, he'd been slow, putting it off until one day it was too late.

He looked over his shoulder and saw smoke in the sky.

With a little luck, Cromwell would be too busy to check the beeves. Fine. They would push the cattle up the limestone ledges until they met the east fork of the Saline, then they'd cut left on the regular trail, where the immigrant traffic would confuse their tracks, hurry them along another ten miles, then they'd be close enough to the Bullseye, where the boy could drive them through the flint hill arroyos, past the ranch. A hidden box canyon on west would hold the cattle until he could get back and change their brands.

Four hours later he knew they'd won. There was no one on their backtrail, and he gave the boy his traveling orders.

"Pa, it ain't right," the boy said nervously, his eyes blinking rapidly.

"Keep 'em movin'. Likely I'll be out tomorrow."

Wayne Askey turned his tired sorrel, put the spurs to him, and rode in a straight line for Ellsworth.

When Dave Cromwell looked across the meadow and saw the cabin reduced to ashes, he knew he'd been too let down. Somehow he'd thought he was finished with the trouble and that the town would kill itself like a rattlesnake biting its tail. For sure he hadn't thought anyone would ride out ahead of them.

He'd wasted too much time in the Drover's Rest, too much time with Eloise, and the stranglers weren't waiting. He'd given them an opening and they'd taken it instantly.

Dave and Lou sat on their horses a moment, gazing at the charred timbers, the iron Spark cookstove and the fallen tin stove pipe. There was nothing else.

"Good thing we moved out last night," Lou said. "I didn't lose anything."

"Wonder why they didn't fire the barn?" Dave asked, and then he saw the flutter of paper on the gatepost of the corral.

Dave handed it over to Lou Wolford to read:

CROMWELL GET OUT OF KANSAS
STRANGLERS

"Low-down polecats!" Dave swore. "I'm ridin' back there and clean out the whole damned bunch."

"Think a minute —" Lou lifted his hand to calm Dave down. "They couldn't have planned this. They looked like ghosts when they saw us ride into town, because they thought we were already dead. This is somethin' else."

"Most anyone using his head and seeing us go in the Drover's Rest at noontime could beat us out here, light it off, and be gone," Dave said more calmly.

"And leave the note. That's what don't set right," Lou said determinedly. "It's an open invitation to fight."

"That's it," Dave said. "They came out here fast, set the fire, and left the warning, knowin' I'd head right back for a showdown."

"Meanin' to get somebody killed," Lou nodded.

"All right, we'll go back, but we're not sayin' anything. We'll play it our way."

"I'm gettin' to know the trail," old Lou smiled. "Let's go."

The sun sat on the western rim, firing the clouds pink and purple, and a lavender haze fell over the endless prairie as the pair once again turned onto First Street from River Road.

As they pulled up in front of the Hotel Ritz, Dave noticed the tired sorrel enter the street from the west but paid it little attention until some drovers caught the horse and stared in horror at the dead man slumped over the saddle.

"He's wired to the saddle!"

"Who is it?"

"Why that's Wayne Askey!"

"That'll be our house burner," Lou Wolford muttered.

*There you go, that's all the chokers you goin' to need tonight!*

"That makes five . . ." Dave Cromwell said softly.

# 6

Roy Abbott, using his ample girth, pushed through the crowd and examined the body. There were the two wires coming together at the back of the neck and twisted tight. No escaping that kind of a noose once it was pulled right.

Abbott felt an icicle probe the back of his own neck and unconsciously reached back and touched the spot. He knew then that there could no longer be any pretense at justice and honor.

He himself had pushed those pinioned men off the bridge, and not only that, he had felt the thrill of power when he did it.

No longer would the rhetoric about law and order and asking justice for a little girl preserve his way of life.

He was on his way to being rich. He'd been buying blocks of land in the platted town, and the prices of lots were going up month by month as the immigrants continued to arrive on the trains, eager to find land and start breaking ground.

It was just a trickle now, but soon whole

colonies of foreigners all the way from Denmark to Portugal would be coming and wanting land. The future was bright, a great fortune was there to be made; all Abbott had to do was stay alive.

Why should young Dave Cromwell want to kill him? Why had he killed the simple townsmen?

Cromwell hadn't been a friend of those crazy cowboys, Curly and Frank. He hadn't been a friend of the redheaded horsethief or that kid rustler.

Yet he'd fought tooth and nail to save them. What was it he'd said before Askey tied the gag — "He's innocent . . ." — not likely. He was in jail. Birds of a feather. Tarred with the same brush. It wasn't the committee's fault.

And there was little Kathy Doran. Someone had to avenge her death, even if it was an accident. Everyone has to pay for their mistakes in this world, and so Curly Dorn and Frank Rostetter had paid. By no stretch of the imagination could they have let those two child killers escape the rope.

If they'd waited for the judge, maybe he'd sent them all to Topeka, and then the lawyers would wrangle back and forth until all the money was gone, and then the death of Kathy Doran would be forgotten.

No, he had nothing on his conscience. Maybe it wasn't legal, maybe it had nothing to do with honor and law, but, by God, they set an example for the cattle camps, and there'd be no backing down now.

"Meet me in the bank in half an hour," he said in a low voice to Gus Fallon, who had taken charge.

"I'll be there," Fallon said without moving his lips, and then yelled at the curious crowd, "Make way, damn it! Somebody get Tom Fancher! Back up, everybody!"

Abbott returned to the store, replaced his apron with his black alpaca coat, then looked in the gun case for a weapon.

He wasn't a gunman, and he knew it was too late to learn. The big forty-fours and forty-fives were too heavy and cumbersome for him to carry. Even the .36-caliber Navy Colt was too much. He settled on the finely made .31-caliber derringer with the two-and-a-half-inch brass barrel. It held only one shot, but how many did a man need?

Making sure it was loaded, he slipped it into an inside pocket and walked out on the boardwalk leaving old Mrs. Soderman to take care of the business. He saw Oakley Hunter coming out of the crowd, scribbling in a notebook.

Intercepting him at the door of the *Record Republican*, he saw that the newspaperman's features were swollen, and the pouches under his eyes were a yellowish grey.

"We're meeting in the bank," Roy Abbott said quietly.

"Not me, Roy, I'm quitting before I end up with a wire around my neck."

"Don't be foolish. You were there. You're one of us," Roy Abbott said angrily.

"No, no. Remember I told you not to do it. . . ."

"You're trying to change the truth and save your skin, but it won't do you any good. Whoever's behind these killings was there that night and knows the real story."

"I tell you, I'm out of it!"

"Fine. You can count on every business in this town withdrawing its advertising from your paper. And when this is all over, you'll wish you'd stayed with us instead of running like a yellow dog," Roy Abbott said angrily.

"Don't threaten me, Abbott. I might just print the whole story with names and all and let you try to explain it away," Hunter spoke loudly.

"Afternoon, gentlemen."

They both froze when they heard a soft

drawl from the hitchrail as Tyson Tuck tied his tall walking horse and came up to the boardwalk.

"I was thinking about advertising some, as business seems to be falling off," Tuck said.

"Falling off?" Roy Abbott looked up into Tuck's genial face. "The town is booming! If you booted out that Dave Cromwell, you'd do a lot better."

"You might be right, Mr. Abbott. Maybe I'm just making excuses," Tuck said. "It's like the lazy young man who wanted a license to preach and told the bishop he'd had a vision of three letters inside a frame. They were GPC. 'Do you know what they mean?' asked the bishop. 'They must mean Go Preach Christ,' the young man declared. 'No, I reckon not,' said the old bishop. 'I think in this case they mean Go Pick Cotton.' "

Even as Tuck chuckled at his own joke, Abbott abruptly turned on his heel and walked off toward the bank, while Oakley Hunter stared after him and muttered abstractedly, "If you want an advertisement, just write it out and bring it in."

"I'll do that, sir," Tuck responded, looking over his head at the retreating storekeeper.

Entering the brick bank building, Roy Abbott forced a set smile on his blocky face, determined to give an air of not only confidence, but the appearance of victory, despite the evidence to the contrary outside in the street.

Phil Meredith looked up from a map of the state of Maine. He was growing tired of this barbarous country even though there were fortunes to be made yet. A quarter of a million dollars in gold and greenbacks lay in his vault, and he felt that it was his more than anyone else's because it was his bank. Never mind that his depositors trusted him, the deep-down morality of the banker was at best shaky.

He'd been thinking that most swindlers and embezzlers always went west to hide, but he'd always like the lobster of Penobscot Bay. If the winters became too cold and boring, he could take a steamship to Cuba or the state of Florida, where it was said to be warm all year round.

Certainly no one would expect him to head east to Maine, or look for him there.

He wanted to liquidate his properties in town and the empty acreage on the Bullfoot that he leased to Dave Cromwell, and then say goodbye very quietly.

Now more than ever was the time to clear out.

From his front window he'd seen the carcass of Wayne Askey go by, a sure signal that the stranglers were marked men.

Slipping the map under the green desk blotter, he rose and made the grimace that passed for a smile and said, "Sit down, Roy. What brings you out?"

"You saw Askey?"

"Indeed. Absolutely unpardonable. We may be next."

"I don't see why. We know that Dave Cromwell is behind these killings — why don't we do something about it?"

"Have you already forgotten Bert Gwinner?" Meredith saw Marshal Fallon entering the bank and rose to greet him.

"Sit down, Marshal," he said with all the friendly warmth he could muster.

"I'll stand. You wanted to talk?" he asked Roy Abbott.

"What about Dave Cromwell?"

"What about him? I'm just glad you didn't invite me to that necktie party that was about as secret as a bullhide hangin' on a fence."

"It was a matter of getting justice," Roy Abbott said, flushing a choleric red.

"You findin' out that the justice knife

130

cuts both ways?" Gus Fallon chuckled meanly.

"The killing must be stopped," Phil Meredith said.

"I don't have any evidence. I can't arrest Cromwell just on suspicions."

"Why not?"

"Why not? I'll tell you why not, Mr. Abbott," Gus Fallon said hotly, "you ain't payin' me enough to risk my neck for your personal quarrel."

"What about Eloise? I thought you had some honorable intentions in mind."

"That's different. Point is, she don't cotton to me, and I ain't about to kiss her foot," Gus said, still angry.

"Suppose you could find a friend that would help you nail Cromwell?"

"There's a Mex that lives over on Railroad Avenue. His name is Ramon Valdez. He'd want a hundred dollars to kill a man."

"That's awfully high," Phil Meredith objected.

"Forget it, then. I don't want no bargain-priced kid guardin' my back."

"Wait, Gus, get your man. We'll have to assess a tax on the seven of us left."

"Better say six. I don't think Reverend Edenfield will pay into this pot," Meredith said in a businesslike way.

"My God, do you realize that nearly half of us are gone!" Roy Abbott was worried.

"What's your plan?" Gus asked. "I haven't agreed to anything yet."

"Cromwell and Wolford are in town, staying at the hotel."

"Why?" Fallon demanded.

"Who knows?" Roy Abbott said. "Suppose Eloise takes him a note from me. He trusts her. Suppose the note said to meet me at the depot at about one o'clock, when no one's around. Suppose you come along and put him under arrest."

"He won't stand for it," Fallon growled.

"Your Mexican friend could be on the roof of the bank just across the street. Say you touch your hat as a signal. You square away to draw. The Mexican shoots Cromwell with a rifle. I'm nearby with this in case he misses —" Roy Abbott pulled out the gleaming brass derringer.

"Catch him in a crossfire," Fallon said. "I like that. Is there a ladder to the roof?"

"At the rear of the building on the alley," Meredith said. "The roofers nailed it permanent."

"I want somethin' extra for myself," Gus Fallon said.

"Don't be too greedy. After all, we're just asking you to arrest a known murderer."

"Mister, I'm not on his list. You are."
Fallon smiled.

"Very well, if you succeed, two hundred to you and one hundred to the sniper."

"You gave Gwinner five hundred and got nothing," Fallon snarled and started for the door. "The hell with it. You can kill your own snakes."

"Wait! Wait!" Roy Abbott called so loudly the clerk in the front of the bank looked up with concern.

"Well?" Fallon turned.

"You have it. Five hundred. We'll meet at the freight platform at one."

"I'll be there." Gus Fallon turned and strode out the door.

"But, Dad, it's not proper for me to take messages to that man," Eloise protested.

"I'm sorry, my dear, but he doesn't trust me, and he trusts you," Roy Abbott said. "You just tell him you want to meet at the depot, where the three of us can talk. That's all there is to it."

"Somehow it doesn't sound right," Eloise said.

"Damn it!" Roy Abbott lost his temper. "Just do it!"

"All right," she acquiesced. "Of course, if you feel that strongly about it."

Accordingly she walked down the board-walk to the Hotel Ritz and asked the clerk if Dave Cromwell was in.

"No, ma'am, he just went over to the Drover's Rest. He has a taste for the lunch there," the clerk replied, bug-eyed that such a beautiful girl should be so forward.

"Is there someone who can deliver a message for me?" She knew that she wasn't permitted to enter the saloon.

"I can do it, it's just two doors down." The young clerk blushed, feeling like a fool.

"Just give him this note, please."

"I'll do it." The clerk nearly fell down in his eagerness.

In less than a minute he returned and said, "I gave it to him, I did."

"Thank you very kindly," she said.

" 'Twasn't nothin'," he stammered, gazing into her lovely eyes.

Dave Cromwell and Lou Wolford had not even started to build their sandwiches, when the youth came rushing in, skidded to a stop, and rushed out the words, "Miss Eloise Abbott wants you to have this." Shoving the envelope into Dave's hand, the boy had rushed out as fast as he'd come in, leaving the regulars smiling in wonderment.

Alvin Hardisty had been playing solitaire, and a couple of older ranchers were settled at a table discussing the cattle market. Tuck was tending bar, and Luis Javier was setting up the platters of free lunch.

"That boy's faster'n a flash of lightnin' through a gooseberry bush," Tuck smiled.

"I reckon she don't know I can't read," Dave said, studying the message. "I'd sure like her to teach me, though."

"Need any help, Dave?" Lou asked.

"Translate that for me, less'n it's too personal," Dave made a wry face.

Studying the message, Lou said, "Says her and her pa want to meet you at the freight platform at one o'clock."

"Does it say why?"

"To make peace." Lou read the final phrase.

"Nothin' I'd like better than some peace. Besides, we got to order a load of lumber down that way."

"Lumber?" Tuck asked casually.

"Goin' to build us a cabin," Dave said matter-of-factly. "Our old one is a little too airy."

Tuck thought on that a moment and murmured, "Burned out?"

"Wasn't much of a loss," Dave said.

"The cattle?" Tuck asked pointedly.

Dave stared at Lou and hit his big fist into his left hand. "Dang it, Lou, we didn't think to go look at the herd."

"Let's ride," Lou said bitterly.

"Right after we pow pow with Roy Abbott and Eloise," Dave said.

"Funny you'd think of that, Tuck, and we didn't."

"I expect you were thinkin' more about your cabin," Tuck smiled. "That's natural."

Feeling heavy from the beer and heavy food, Dave wouldn't have minded a five-minute siesta, but the Regulator clock on the wall said it was ten to one.

"I reckon a little walk might settle down that good roast beef," he murmured.

"That note didn't mention anyone wantin' to make peace with me," old Lou muttered. "You just go on ahead and watch sharp."

Walking down First Street, Dave observed that most of the businesses were closed for the noon hour and that the main life in the street was a couple of dogs chasing pigeons.

At Telegraph Avenue where the brick bank building stood, he crossed over, then turned left toward the depot.

The freight platform was a broad deck built of scarred timbers and was half full of unclaimed freight from new ploughs to steamer trunks. There was no sheltering roof here. On down at the depot and telegraph office, there was a roof extending almost clear to the tracks, but that was for people on rainy days. Freight was expected to be rainproof.

As he climbed the three steps to the freight platform, he saw Eloise and her father approaching from the other way.

*Fine. Right on time,* he thought.

He waited on the platform, looking off to the left and right. From the right sauntered the black-clad Gus Fallon, acting as if he were just out on patrol. Coming from the left across the tracks, Dave saw the flat-topped hat of Alvin Hardisty moving this way.

"Hello, Dave," Eloise said in a calm, sweet voice. "How are you?"

"I'm movin' ahead, Eloise," he said, feeling weak as he looked into the dark blue of her eyes.

"Mr. Cromwell, I've come to make peace," Roy Abbott said, smiling like a bear in a bee tree. "I hope you feel the same way."

"I ain't been doin' nothin' exceptin'

mindin' my own business," Dave said. "Let's say you don't burn down my house no more, and I won't burn down yours."

"Your house?" Eloise asked anxiously.

"It was just a box to batch in," Dave said. "I been wantin' a real house where I could raise a family someday."

"But can you afford it?" she asked.

"I got five hundred dollars cash money." Dave's eyes slanted wickedly toward Roy Abbott.

"Why not!" Roy Abbott declared enthusiastically as Gus Fallon came up the steps.

"Howdy, folks," he said, failing to touch his hat when he nodded to Eloise.

*Funny,* thought Dave, *he did before. Everybody does.*

"Look, Dave, there's been too much killin'," Gus said quietly.

"I second the motion," Dave said, "but I have nothin' to do with any of it."

Roy Abbott had quietly taken his daughter's wrist in his left hand and moved backwards.

"Wait, dad —" she exclaimed, puzzled.

"We'll talk later," Roy Abbott said.

"But we came here to talk —" she protested.

"No, ma'am," Dave said, suddenly alert

as he saw the trap, "you come to put me away."

"Now look, Dave," Gus Fallon said, his hand going to his hat brim as if to wipe the sweat off his brow, "just come over to the jail where we can get to the bottom of all this."

The gesture to the hat was false, Dave knew. Gus was a bad actor. The whole thing was a setup.

Dave backed toward the pile of freight, his hand covering his six-gun. "Get clear, Eloise," he said as he abruptly dropped to his knees behind a crate marked Pick Handles.

Two shots sounded as one and a bullet whined by his ear as he dropped, then rolled to one side, as both Gus Fallon and Roy Abbott drew their pistols and fired.

Eloise was in his line of fire, rendering Dave helpless. He couldn't fight with her standing right where anyone's bullet might go.

He went rolling amongst the heavy crates as a volley of bullets screamed and gunsmoke hazed over the street, until he knelt at the rear of the platform. If he were to leap off into the vacant lot behind, he'd make a wide open target.

"Get the girl out!" he yelled, "and I'll fight you!"

A bullet skipped off a moldboard plough and pinged heavenward.

From a distance, he heard a rifle fire, and suddenly, Marshal Fallon went down.

Without him, there was no fight in Roy Abbott. Keeping his daughter close, he backed away to the street, and they were gone.

With his Colt .44 at the ready, Dave worked his way through the freight to where he could see Fallon sitting on the deck, his revolver holstered, so that he could hold his right foot in both hands with a grimace of pain on his face.

"You all right, Marshal?" came the voice of Lou Wolford from the side.

"Somebody shot the heel off my boot," Gus Fallon cursed. "I think it broke my ankle."

"Lucky shot," Lou said coming into the open. "It could have been higher, and they'd a called you hoppy ever after."

"What's goin' on?" Dave asked, coming out into the open.

"I don't know why you cut down on me," Fallon bluffed, "I was only tryin' to talk some sense into you."

"Sense?"

"Just doin' my job."

"That include bushwhackin', Marshal?" Lou asked mildly.

"I don't know what you mean — I was talkin' and this ranny all of a sudden drops down and starts a fight."

"I never fired a shot," Dave said quietly. "What kind of a setup was it, Lou?"

"They was a man planted on the roof of the bank just yonder," Lou nodded toward the bank. "Happened I seen him as I was astrollin' along, tryin' to settle my dinner, and kind of barked him like a squirrel in a tree."

"Where is he now?" Marshal Fallon asked weakly.

"I reckon he's still layin' in the alley, I didn't watch after the first bounce."

"That was it," Dave nodded, smiling, "I heard somethin' and ducked. Started a fight that I didn't mean to. I apologize, Marshal. Tell Mr. Abbott and his lovely daughter that I apologize for my nervousness."

Fallon looked at the tall cowboy suspiciously, "I don't get you."

"I been a little snorty lately," Dave said placidly, "so when I heard a rifle hammer cock and a shot comin' my way, I naturally ducked. Then you folks thought I was for shootin' you, so it got to be a real mixup. A good thing nobody was hurt."

"Except I need a new pair of boots," Gus

Fallon growled, confused by the light attitude of the man he wanted to kill. He couldn't very well draw on him sitting down, and even standing up it was a fifty-fifty chance, and Marshal Fallon never went past a hundred-to-one.

"Come on, Lou, maybe we better tally the stock," Dave said.

Together they walked back up the street, hardly speaking, but once mounted and riding out River Road, Dave said, "How come you walkin' down alleys at noontime?"

"Wasn't my idea exactly, give Tuck credit. He just kind of suggested there'd be a backshooter around in that neighborhood."

"That Tuck is sure some sort of a wizard," Dave grinned. "That's twice he's saved my bacon."

They rode into the ranch from the River Road. Nothing had changed, except the wind had carried the ashes of the cabin farther away.

"I'll bet the stockers are just over that hill," Lou said.

"What'll you bet?"

"Whoever loses is the cook next week," Lou grinned.

"I hate to bet against myself," Dave said

as they rode up the hill. "Make it a nickel."

"God hates a coward," Lou said.

"All right, but just remember, you called it." Dave smiled, and as they skylined the hill, his smile faded away to sheer wonder.

"Nothin' there."

"Reckon I owe you a nickel," Lou said, spurring on over the hill down into the lowland, studying the tracks as he went.

"I'll be goddamned!" He stopped his bay and studied the sign.

"You see a diamond mine or somethin'?"

"Look at them tracks." Old Lou smiled.

"They look like a stampede of buffaloes to me," Dave said, unable to sort out the many tracks imprinted in the damp ground.

"Cattle."

"See them."

"Two horses."

"I see horse tracks, maybe one or ten."

"One's a ribby mustang with a light rider," old Lou said carefully, "but the other is mighty interestin'."

"I sure hope you don't want to bet on that," Dave said, deadpan, waiting for the old man to reveal his discovery.

"Well, it goes back to when we seen Wayne Askey's sorrel walkin' in. I noticed the crooked shoe then. Probably set it himself and said the hell with it."

"Same print. Same sorrel. Means . . ."

"Means Askey stole the stock," Lou said.

"Him and somebody else."

"Probably a kid," Lou nodded.

"Let's track 'em down."

Letting Lou lead the way, Dave, on Coalie, followed the tracks easily seen until they came to the Bullfoot, which had carved its bed down to limestone bedrock.

"One of us rides downstream, the other up," Dave said. "They got to come out somewhere."

"Sure enough. But you won't see nothin' in the dark."

*Of course,* Dave thought, *Lou thinks of everything, including sunset.*

Already the lavender haze was creeping across the prairie as the sun settled in the west.

"Daybreak, then," Dave said and turned Coalie for the barn.

# 7

That evening when George Philbrick swept the floor of the barbershop, mingling the grey, the yellow, the red, and the brown locks he had shorn during the day, he saw himself in the sweepings. His life, he thought, was little more than a pile of dead, dirty hair.

He had wanted to be something when he was young, wanted to overcome the poverty brought on by the death of his father at Antietam. Wanted to give his mother a carriage and four white horses, but even in school, he'd had the fear of failure and learned to cover it with a joke and artificial laughter.

When he'd been called to the big slate blackboard to do multiplication, he couldn't remember what eight times nine was. He guessed wrong, then wiggled his ears and laughed. The class thought it was funny, but the teacher rapped him on the head with an oak yardstick.

In Cincinnati he'd tried, really tried, he thought morosely, remembering his mother and little sister trying to keep some gentility in their lives while helplessly watching it erode away. But he'd tried.

He'd shined boots, worked nights in a restaurant, and gotten up before daybreak to hawk apples and his mother's sandwiches at the train station, but every time he made a nickel, there was the hand of the landlord or the groceryman or the doctor reaching out for it.

He'd even tried dancing and singing in the Grand Western Saloon, but he was tone deaf and his voice was cracking so that it embarrassed the clients. Once he'd wiggled his ears, crossed his eyes, and made rubbery faces by sucking in his cheeks, he'd run out of things to do.

His sister, seeing the handwriting on the wall, married a railway brakeman, and started having babies. His mother's health was declining, and George wanted to make a million dollars for her so that she could recover in luxury with servants and proper doctors, but he couldn't.

Once the TB found her, she went mercifully fast, leaving George Philbrick brokenhearted, because he felt that he had failed again, failed his own beloved mother.

It was only natural that he would, at the age of eighteen, make his way west to St. Louis, but it was only incidental luck that

146

he found a job cleaning a large tonsorial emporium with eight chairs and eight journeyman barbers dressed in white smocks.

The place was lined with big mirrors and the floor was made of gleaming white tile. At each chair was a sink with running water, and over the sink was a shelf crowded with bottles of hair tonic, creams, oils, and shampoos. Here the rich men of St. Louis came each day to be trimmed, shaven, and anointed while their boots were being shined and their fingernails filed and polished.

It was a grand place for a poor young boy to work and imagine that someday he might own a similar establishment all shining and spotless. After a year of close association with the barbers, he was given the chair at the end where the transient drummers might come if every other chair were full.

He'd had to buy his hand clippers, comb, scissors, Lucky Tiger Tonic, razor, and strop out of his wages, so that he never seemed to get ahead.

Still, he smiled and laughed a lot and learned new jokes, wiggled his ears, rolled his eyes, and in general made himself funny for the rich men.

By the time he'd moved up to the third chair from the end, he wore a natty new suit off work, and he could take a girl on the excursion boat if there was a holiday, or to a beer garden where they all sang "Sweet Adeline" or "The Little Mohee" and danced a polka or waltzed close together.

He'd found a merry Irish lass who worked in a loft, making shirtwaists for very little money, and they planned to be married as soon as they could afford it. She was achingly beautiful, with a swelling bosom and grand haunch, but then all of a sudden she was pregnant, and he had to learn that two don't live as cheaply as one.

That was his downfall, he reflected. He'd had a future up until they were married. Should have run for San Francisco and started over. Should have thrown her in the river. Should never have run his hand up her leg.

Thought you were such a rare bird, plundering the sweet little girl! The ecstasy! Couldn't get enough of it.

One baby and the sweet little girl became a porky, unkempt wife with a temper. Always blaming him!

He'd provided as best he could, better than a lot of other men he knew, but she could throw more away with a spoon than he could bring home with a wagon.

Then he'd fallen. Made the second big

mistake. What is eight times nine? Seventy-one? Is a decent job worth the chance of stealing a diamond stickpin? Yes, if you can get away with it.

But he'd been confronted by the shop owner himself the next morning. Either fork over Mr. Astorbilt's diamond stickpin or go to jail. You be honest and give it back. What do you get?

You get canned.

By then they had three noisy kids and another on the way.

Without references, he couldn't find another job, and in desperation, while they still could borrow a few dollars, they'd headed for the frontier and landed at the end of the line.

Ellsworth had been good enough. He made a fair living, but he knew he'd never go any farther than one chair in a shop he leased from the banker. At the end of every day for the rest of his life he'd sweep the varicolored hair on the floor into a scoop, take it out on the boardwalk, and toss it into the street, where it would blow away.

There was some kind of a profound idea in this, he thought, but his mind couldn't find it. He looked in the mirror, saw the jack-o'-lantern, rubbery face going downhill, wiggled his ears, rolled his eyes, sucked in his cheeks, and thought, *Well, Georgie, that's life.*

But as he made faces at the mirror, he caught a glimpse of another strange face. It appeared and disappeared so fast, he wasn't sure. Someone out in the street had looked through the window for just a moment, then gone. Why?

Fear overpowered his funny front. He went to the window, peering out carefully, but saw no one. The town was finished for the day except for the cowboys trailing into the Red Dog and a few of the cleaner type going on up to the Drover's Rest.

He tried to remember that sudden vision, but it remained vague and blurred in his recollection. Maybe it was the man with the lengths of baling wire, that angel of vengeance.

Normally he didn't carry a gun, but he kept an old Colt Dragoon that weighed about as much as an anvil in a drawer. He brought it out and saw that it was loaded, then wrapped it in an old *Record Republican* so that it resembled a harmless package.

Pulling the shades, he went out the door, locked it behind him, looked both ways, then moved down the darkened street.

Passing by the Drover's Rest, he heard Luis Javier Fajardo playing the accordion and singing. He wanted very much to go in and have a drink and join the company of men, but he was afraid.

Looking over his shoulder, he turned up River Road to Fourth Street, then went left half a block to the small frame house that he called home.

He would be safe there.

Inside, his porcine wife was sitting at the table eating pancakes, and the four kids were howling like Indians.

"Pancakes for supper!" he yelled. "And you didn't even wait for me!"

"Why should I wait on you?" she growled belligerently. "Just tell me why I shouldn't have pancakes when there's nothing else to eat in the house, and tell me why I should wait for the provider of nothing!"

"Provider of nothing? What did you do with that ten dollars I gave you this morning?"

"If you must know, I went down to Roy Abbott's store and bought ten bottles of Golden Vigor of Life as well as a pair of high-buttoned shoes, and if you must know, two pairs of ladies drawers."

"Size forty-eight," he said thickly, enraged, and frustrated. The kids building forts out of the rickety furniture, the dog sneaking out the back door with a ham bone.

"Take it or leave it," she said, uncaring.

"How can I leave it!" he cried out. "You waste every cent I make. We're always in debt. We're never going to get out of this town. I could make good in San Francisco!"

"No more," she laughed. "No, funny man, your feet are flat, your knees are gone, and nobody laughs at your act anymore. What you better do is jack up your prices so we can live like everybody else in this godawful town!"

"I'm finished," he yelled. "Count me out! I'm leaving!"

"Go on," she said, taking a swig from the bottle of patent medicine laced with alcohol. "You'll be back with your tail between your legs."

"You're wrong this time!"

"I could wish," she said as he flung himself out the door.

Hurrying up to River Road, he turned back toward First Street. As he was about to enter the Drover's Rest, he remembered he'd put the Dragoon on a shelf in the kitchen cupboard. He hoped none of the kids would find it. Of course, if they happened to shoot that old sow of a wife, it would be a blessing for all.

Smiling at that, he went through the door and headed for the bar which, though not three-deep in raging cowboys, was still comfortably full. There was even some of the free lunch left, and he felt starved.

"A beer first. A beer for good cheer!" He smiled at Tuck. "Did you ever hear about the granger who went to the show? The usher asked him if he wanted to sit down in front. The granger looked at the usher as if he was crazy, and said, 'Look, mister, I don't bend that way.'"

Tuck laughed and said, "You're sure a funny one, Mr. Philbrick."

Alvin Hardisty, who stood next to him, chuckled, and Tuck said, "I recall the granger who put a chair in his coffin for rigor mortis to set in."

At daybreak Dave and Lou rode across the bottom land, aiming for Bullfoot Creek, where they had stopped the night before. They carried scabbarded short rifles and their usual six-guns, and a sack of johnny cakes, enough to keep them going for two days.

"They wouldn't take 'em downstream," Dave said. "It'd just put 'em back towards town. Better we both push upstream and save time."

"Makes sense."

Accordingly they turned left up the limestone-bedded stream and walked their horses through the shallow water.

They saw skid marks on the steep bank where a steer had tried to climb out and then slipped back down again.

"That settles it, for sure," Lou nodded.

"I think maybe old Askey figured we'd be dead by now from unnatural causes and took his inheritance a little early."

They proceeded on for another mile until the stream made a bow and the banks evened off into a small flood plain where the immigrant trail forded the stream and went on west.

"Likely they'd move 'em out here," Lou said, studying the tracks of wagons, horses, cattle, and sheep. "There's his track. He's westering."

Dave lifted the black into a slow gallop along the broad, level trail with Lou's bay matching his stride.

Lou stayed to the far right, where he could see if a small herd turned off, and Dave stayed to the far left for the same reason.

After a mile they slowed the horses to a walk and let them take a breather, then galloped another mile before dropping back to a walk again. Dave didn't want to run into a fight on a tired horse, nor did he want to damage the strong animal by foolishly driving him too hard.

After some six miles of this disciplined riding, Dave asked, "Could we have missed their turnoff?"

"No, I don't think so," Lou replied. "For all we know, they're drivin' 'em to Denver."

"No. Askey must have left the herd and started back to town, when he got himself killed."

"Could be they handed 'em over to another bunch of rustlers," Lou suggested.

"To make the times fit, seems like we ought to be pretty close to where Askey left the herd."

Hardly had he spoken than he heard voices ahead.

Both riders pulled up, then silently reined off to one side and waited.

Coming around a curve in the trail, the herd of two-year-olds moved at a fast walk. A lad on a horse rode on the right flank, keeping them to the trail, while another barefoot youngster on the left walked quickly along carrying a switch made of a willow branch.

The brand was Circle C.

"What do you make of it?" Lou asked quietly.

"They're bringin' them back."

"That's crazy."

"Maybe not, with Askey dead," Dave said and galloped across the drag where a small boy walked, throwing rocks at the lazy ones. When Dave came on around without spooking the cattle, the boy on the paint mustang stopped and held up his hands.

Dave saw that he was a thin youngster about fifteen years old. He was scared, but he had made up his mind to hold his ground.

"Who are you?" Dave asked flatly.

"I'm Caspar Askey."

"Wayne's son?"

"Yes, sir. They sent a rider out last night and told Ma he was killed."

"So you decided to bring back the cattle?"

"Yes, sir, Mr. Cromwell, I was against takin' them and against burnin' you out, but I couldn't go against Pa."

"These your brothers?"

"Yessir. We'uns got a hardscrabble ranch off there in the Flint Hills."

"What'll you do now your dad's gone?"

"I don't rightly know. I'm hopin' you don't hang me first. If I can get past that, I'll look for work and help Ma out."

"You got any other help out there?"

"My brothers are big enough to take my place."

"Send your brothers on home and ride with us back to the Circle C. We can cut across the prairie and save some time."

The boy took the drag, the men took the flanks, and in three hours they put the herd back on the lush bottom land.

Dave passed around the johnny cakes and looked at Caspar. Everything he owned was patched. His saddle was wired together, the bridle reins were made of cotton rope. His shoes were broken, and he didn't own a hat. He tried to eat in a reserved way, but the johnny cakes seemed to disappear like smoke.

Clearly the boy was half starved.

"Caspar . . ." Dave started.

"Most folks call me Cappy."

"Cappy, I'm sorry about your dad. I had nothin' to do with his death, and neither did Lou."

"I know that. It couldn't have been you, because you'd be here at the ranch. I'm sure glad the barn didn't catch."

"Me too," Dave said. "You think your ma can spare you for a job with us?"

"Yessir, I'd be proud to work for you, Mr. Cromwell." Cappy's face flushed and his eyes looked straight into Dave's.

"All right, you go on home now and get it straight with your mom. Come back

157

Monday by way of Ellsworth. Can you write?"

"No, sir."

"Me neither," Dave said grimly. "Lou, write out an order to the Mercantile. Say to outfit Caspar from top to bottom and charge it to me."

"I'll earn it back, Mr. Cromwell." Cappy was near tears.

"Might as well call me Dave, Cappy." Dave smiled. "Now, if I was you, I'd find your dad's horse and saddle and use them, and you ought to talk to your ma about sellin' whatever tack and harness he left in the shop."

"I'll do that, Dave." Rising, he said to Lou, "I just don't hardly know how to thank you all."

"Get outa here," old Lou growled deadpan, "before we change our minds and stretch your neck."

After Cappy had ridden off west, Dave murmured, "Funny how an ornery stud can throw a good colt."

"It happens."

"Maybe we can both learn to read and write next winter," Dave said wistfully, thinking of Eloise Abbott.

"Likely."

"I wonder if she knew she was bait

158

for her dad's trap?"

"Who?" Lou asked, his face expressionless.

"Who?" Dave laughed and threw his hat at the old man. "Who do you think, who?"

"Well, I'd say it's funny how an ornery stud can throw a good filly too."

Eloise Abbott was pacing back and forth in the ample kitchen as her mother ladled sauerkraut from a crock and set it to heat on the nickel-plated stove. From another crock she fished out a pickled pork butt and cut the chunk into thick slices, adding them to the pot of sauerkraut.

"Cut the bread, will you, Eloise?" she asked, breaking Eloise out of her worried reverie.

"Do you think Daddy would deliberately try to kill Dave, Mom?"

"Not unless he thought he had to protect us from something worse."

"Something awfully strange's going on in this town." Eloise attacked the loaf of wheat bread with a sharp butcher knife. "And Daddy seems to be right in the middle of it."

"It's the way he is. He likes to be the head man," her mother said in a low voice, looking over her shoulder fearfully.

"But did he have anything to do with the strangler's committee?"

"You can't believe the gossip," her mother said curtly. "You just have to live day by day and do the best you can."

"But he had that little gun and was ready to kill Dave for nothing."

"I suppose he's got some plan we aren't privy to. Anyway, he's the head of the family, and we'll do well to just keep him happy and stay out of his way."

"But Mother, so many men are being killed! And it's all men, not women. There's some plan back of it."

"I just watch my own backyard, young lady." Her mother frowned. "You mustn't upset your father with a lot of wild talk."

"But then how can we truly help him?"

"I told you. See he's content in his own home."

"But what about us, you and I? Don't we count for anything?"

"No. Remember that," she said firmly. "The answer is, we don't count for nothing."

"And if I marry, I'll be the slave of my husband?"

"That's not the right word. I think they call it 'chattel.'" Her mother's voice was bitter. "Best you can do is make sure you find a man with some understanding in his heart."

"Why can't I find a man with some love in his heart?" Eloise cried out. "Daddy keeps pushing that Gus Fallon on me as if he can tell me who I should love and who I should marry."

"With your father's help, I suppose Mr. Fallon could be a success in this town. He's got everyone buffaloed already."

"He hasn't got Dave Cromwell buffaloed. Not by a long shot. Dave humbled him and Daddy both. I never saw men so mad, like they were wild tigers in a cage, but Dave held them down."

"You sound like you're getting mighty sweet on that cowboy."

"He's not a cowboy, he's a rancher."

"Gossip has it that his ranch was burned down and his cattle stolen."

"Oh, no!"

Just then she heard the front door open and footsteps. She went out to the parlor and saw her father closing the door after Gus Fallon.

"Hello."

"Hello, Eloise," her father said. "I brought Gus home to supper. Set an extra plate, please."

"Certainly," she said distractedly.

161

Gus Fallon was scrubbed, shaved, in a clean black outfit, and he smelled of bay rum hair tonic.

"My, how pretty you look tonight," Gus said with a smile, but she saw no warmth in his eyes to match the smile.

"Please sit down, I'll tell Mom you're here," she said, suddenly frightened, and turned quickly back into the kitchen.

"There's plenty extra," her mother said when she heard of the extra guest.

"I'm afraid, Mother," Eloise said, hugging herself. "I get cold chills when I see that man."

"Don't fight it, Eloise. I did once, but then I learned a woman can't win. Best she can do is stay off to one side and do what she's told to do."

"Not me," Eloise said, her jaw firming. "I'm going to live my own life, no matter what."

Supper was a simple enough light evening meal, but Eloise's mother stayed standing in the background making sure the men lacked for nothing. Eloise tried to join her and help with the serving, but her father said, "Sit down, Eloise, eat."

She did as she was told, never looking up from her plate.

"Cat got your tongue, Eloise?" Roy

Abbott asked, a touch of iron in his voice. "Can't you say a kind word to Marshal Fallon?"

"Yes, Daddy, I'm sorry. It's been such nice weather, hasn't it, Mr. Fallon."

"Indeed it has, Eloise," Gus said. "Not a cloud in the sky."

"How long have you been in Ellsworth, Mr. Fallon?"

"About three months now."

"Do you like it here?"

"Yes, very much, except it's a kind of lonely for a man my age."

"Where did you come from?" she asked, hurriedly getting away from that subject.

"El Paso, Laredo, Fort Brown — border towns," Gus said uncomfortably.

"I've heard there are many outlaws along the border," she said.

"There's some, but they ain't so bad once they learn to respect you," Gus chuckled. "They learned quick down there not to cross old Gus Fallon."

"And what did you do for a living there, Mr. Fallon?" she asked, maintaining the impression that she was a lady interested in his life.

"I'm good with cards," Gus said shortly, "and guns. That's about all a man needs down that way."

"Or anywhere else on the frontier," Roy Abbott said jovially.

"More corned pork?" Mrs. Abbott asked from behind Abbott's chair.

"Of course."

"More meat and less kraut for me," Gus said.

Mrs. Abbott took their bowls into the kitchen and returned shortly, serving the men again.

"More bread," Abbott said, spooning up a mess of hot kraut.

Mrs. Abbott hurried back into the kitchen.

Eloise was seeing for the first time in her life how curt her father was with her mother, how unkind he was. He'd not said that the kraut she had laboriously made herself was delicious with the dried apples she added to it. He hadn't said the meat was tender and extra tasty because of the cloves and peppercorns she'd put in the brine, just "do this, do that."

She had lived with it so closely all her life, and yet this was the first time she saw that she would be treated the same way unless she did something to change the course of her life.

She glanced at her father and saw that he was concentrating on shoveling the food into his mouth, hardly pausing to chew before swallowing it down. She looked surreptitiously at Gus and saw that he, too, was a fast eater and that he held the handle of the spoon in his hand like a dagger. Juice dripped onto the napkin tucked in his collar. There was coarse black hair on the back of his hands and fingers.

"Eloise —" her father growled.

"I'm sorry, Daddy, I was thinking about all the trouble in town," she said, feeling her way to a new path in the family.

"It's just the drovers," her father said. "Soon there'll be nothing but permanent settlers on small farms. We'll all be the better for that."

"But how soon is soon?" she asked. "How near is peace and quiet for Ellsworth?"

"A year or two," her father said.

"Then I better get mine while the gettin's good," smiled Gus Fallon.

"But can you ever have peace and quiet that is built on murder?" she asked quietly.

"There's a maniac loose," her father said shortly. "He doesn't have any place in this country. When we catch him we'll stretch his neck and make this town safe for women and children."

"But he's killing men, not women and children. He's killing townspeople . . .

businessmen," she said, probing, trying to garner a kernel of truth from the two.

"Not for long," Gus said. "I'll wool the lightning out of that hombre soon enough."

"Listen, girl," her father said, his pig eyes searching her face, "you let the menfolk worry about such matters. You just tend to embroiderin' the sheets for your hope chest."

"I want nothing to do with hope chests," she declared suddenly. "I prefer to be a spinster school teacher where I can at least teach and change things."

"What is this?" her father growled, now fully engaged in the dispute with her.

"It's just that as a dutiful wife, I'd be helpless to make the world better. As a teacher, I can influence the minds of boys and girls and perhaps change things."

"Change what?" Her father's voice was menacing now, and she was ready to run, but still she persisted.

"To change the way men think that women are nothing more than servants."

"You may be excused," her father said. "We can discuss this later."

When she had retreated to the kitchen, she stared out the window at the dark, hopeless, implacable world and wept into her hands.

"Forgive my daughter's manners, Marshal," Roy Abbott said.

"Don't worry about it," Gus Fallon grinned wolfishly, "I've broke a few wild ones, and there's nothin' I like better'n a spirited filly."

By its very force, a hammering at the front door broke into the thoughts of everyone in the house, and Mrs. Abbott hurried to the door.

"Evenin', missus," Tom Fancher croaked. "Roy in?"

"Come in, please."

Tom Fancher's face was mottled red and dead white. His breath came hard and quick.

Roy Abbott, followed by the marshal, met him in the parlor. Seeing the pair together, Fancher's eyes slitted suspiciously. "Glad I caught you both so cozy . . ."

"What is it, man?" Roy Abbott had had enough challenges to his authority for one day.

"If you didn't know, George Philbrick has been strangled."

Even as he spoke he noticed Abbott's clean-shaven pink jowls and freshly trimmed and singed hair.

# 8

Gus Fallon led the way and was the first to see a few people gathered on the dark boardwalk peering into the lamp-lighted barbershop window.

"Move it out, move it out," he said roughly, jostling Charlie Damker and Alvin Hardisty aside.

Roy Abbott and Tom Fancher arrived, followed by Tuck, Oakley Hunter, and Reverend Edenfield.

"Boil me for a sheep," Oakley Hunter said, "if that ain't the damnedest —"

Sitting in his barber chair, George Philbrick faced the window. They could see that the wire that ran around his neck was twisted to the headrest, holding him up. But it was his face that froze them — greenish yellow and blank-eyed, his mouth set in a broad, grimacing grin, as though the rictus of death had presented him his most grotesque joke.

Draped across his chest was a piece of white cardboard with rough printing.

"What does it say?" Charlie Damker's

rheumy eyes searched out a meaning, letter by letter.

"It says, 'hang 'em all.' " Oakley Hunter's voice trembled. "Remember his poem?"

"Not exactly . . ." Charlie Damker's voice was bleary from his nightly ration of Squaw whiskey.

"He kept repeating it afterward, like he thought it was real funny."

"He recited something tonight . . ." Tuck said softly.

"Hang 'em all," Oakley Hunter quoted angrily. "The big and the small, hang 'em all, the long and the tall, and if they're still in pain, hang 'em all over again . . ."

"My God," Tom Fancher said, "you think it means . . . you think it means what I think it means?"

"I think it means somebody intends to hang everyone in on that lynching," Alvin Hardisty said. "If I was one of 'em, I'd be scattin' out of here like a scalded cat."

"God rest his soul," intoned Reverend Edenfield, his rubicund features soft as a boy's.

"That makes six," Roy Abbott muttered. "Oakley, I think we should have a little talk. You too, Charlie, and Tom, and the reverend."

169

"Look," Charlie Damker said bitterly, "it ain't no secret. Can't you see that? So we put sacks over our heads, still somebody knows we all did it. There's six down and us six to go."

"Shut up!" Roy Abbott swung a fist at Damker's head, knocking him down.

"You're crazy!" Damker continued as if nothing had happened. "He knows! He could be one of us. I'm bettin' it's you, Roy Abbott, you got the most to lose."

"I said, shut up!" Abbott bulled forward and would have kicked Charlie Damker in the face had not Alvin Hardisty moved in between.

"No call for that," Hardisty said.

"I just want to say I'm sorry about it," Damker cried out. "I thought they was four wild ones and no loss to anybody. And whoever you are, don't kill me for somethin' I didn't mean to do!"

"Put him in jail," Roy Abbott said to the marshal. "He's drunk and crazy, out of his head."

"Whoever you are, don't strangle me with that wire!" Damker screamed.

Gus Fallon lifted the flimsily built Damker to his feet. "Come on, you can sober up in jail."

"Passin' strange," Tuck said as the marshal dragged the weeping Damker across the street to the jail.

"How's that?" Alvin Hardisty asked.

"That big grin on his face," Tuck said. "Like he was glad to be goin'."

"They's a new lumberyard over at Lincoln. It ain't much farther from here than Ellsworth," Lou said as Dave worked over a crude plan for the new cabin, trying to make a list of materials.

"I do get the feelin' those Ellsworth folks don't want our business," Dave said.

"Make that cabin plenty big." Old Lou was watching young Cappy riding toward the corral on the sorrel, all in blue except for his hat and new boots, looking like a different person, taller, straighter, broader in the shoulder.

"Boy's comin' along well," Dave said, drawing a picture of a four-paned window and writing a 4 next to it.

"He's good with the horses. Learns quick," Lou nodded. "I been talkin' with him some."

"Have him harness up a team to the wagon and we can be on our way."

"Who goes?"

"You and me. Cappy can work with the green stock. Gentle those hammerheads down some."

171

As Lou went over to the corral, where half a dozen wild horses watched with their ears pointed forward and heads up, Dave continued making his marks on the tablet. He could cipher well enough, it was just the words that he couldn't make sense of.

*Why did he say make the cabin big,* he wondered idly. *Only reason to make it big would be for extra people. And who would they be?* — *Eloise!* Sure, the old fox, always thinking ahead, only this time it was more wish than real, more feathers than chicken.

He couldn't even show his face in Ellsworth without somebody wanting to shoot him. How could he ever court the girl? Besides, she seemed to have some kind of arrangement with Fallon. Hard to believe. If he could just have a talk with her alone without anyone butting in, maybe he could explain how he was just getting started and it was too hard a life right now for a young lady, but maybe in a year or two, the place would be on its feet and they could think about sharing it out.

Maybe Lou was right. Make it bigger. Add another eight feet to the front room that was the kitchen, dining room, office, bathhouse, and parlor, all in one.

The boy came up with a half-green team of four heavy-shouldered mustangs harnessed to a flatbed wagon with wide-tread wheels.

"You can drive," Dave said to Lou. "I'll ride Coalie."

"Think I can hold 'em?" Lou asked Cappy.

"Yessir, unless a rabbit or rattlesnake jumps up under 'em sudden-like."

"I reckon they'll be broke by the time we bring back a wagonload of lumber," Dave said, mounting the black. "If you have time, see if you can work out the kinks in the green stock. There's a kicker in the bunch."

"Just don't try ridin' any of them buckers without somebody around to pick up the pieces," Lou said, and then he lifted the reins, shook them gently, and headed the team northerly, with Dave riding near the head just in case they stampeded. They were rough horses and resented the harness, but they were strong, and with a little patience they'd soon be willing.

Alone, Cappy looked around the yard in front of the barn and expanded his vision to include the prairie all the way to the horizon. It was empty except for scattered bunches of Circle C cows. The prairie wind bent the tall grass and sang its sad melody of time and loneliness, and the boy shivered a moment as the wind's lament penetrated his bones.

Shaking himself loose, he slipped through the rails of the corral and shook out his lass rope. Half a dozen wild horses were backed into a corner, facing him with ears cocked.

"So now," he said softly, and following the lessons he'd learned from old Lou, he kept his loop small and didn't twirl it over his head, because it would spook these mustangs and he'd never catch nothing.

But walking slowly toward them, talking horse talk to them, he came close before they broke like autumn leaves in a wind and swirled about him, snorting and grunting.

A roan came by and kicked out at him so fast he almost didn't dodge in time. Going on by, the roan kicked two other horses in the ribs.

"Well, that's one that needs the kick taken out of him." Cappy smiled and waited until the kicking roan came by again. When the roan threw a rear leg back and snapped its hoof at him, he dabbed the noose over his head and quickly dallied the rope around the snubbing post. The roan reared back, bringing the noose tight around its throat. As he fell forward,

Cappy took up the slack. Again the roan threw himself back against the rope that was tight around his windpipe, cutting off his air.

In a couple of minutes he fell helplessly near the snubbing post and the boy quickly tied his front legs together and then his hind legs.

Choked down to semiconsciousness, the mustang lay on his side, whipped for the moment.

Quickly, Cappy took a short length of steel chain lying by the post, and using a piece of leather piggin' string, he tied the chain to the off rear fetlock.

Satisfied that the chain was secured, he slipped a heavy leather halter over the roan's head, buckled the throatstrap tight, then ran a heavy cotton rope through the ring in the chinstrap on around the roan's neck and tied a bowline which couldn't slip and choke the horse once he was up on his feet.

Satisfied that his gear was in place and fitted right, Cappy released the rear legs, then the front legs, and lastly slacked his lass rope, slipping the noose over the roan's head, freeing him.

Gradually the roan got his breath and his strength back and in a moment sprang to his feet plain-out mad.

Cappy backed off and watched the roan drag the cotton halter rope around the corral, stepping on it once in a while and jerking his neck. Every time he set to kick at another horse, the chain first snapped him in the belly, and then as he kicked, the chain would snap his upper leg.

"You're learnin' all kinds of lessons," Cappy said to him as the roan discovered that if he stepped on the lead rope, his neck would get a shock, and if he kicked, he'd get a couple of shocks.

In hardly any time at all the roan could hang his head sidewise so that he didn't step on the rope and he had quit kicking. Patiently, Cappy watched until he was pretty sure the roan had a knowledge of the halter and understood the thick cotton rope wasn't put there to hurt him. Walking into the corral, he picked up the dragging lead line and took a turn around the snubbing post, tying the roan so that he couldn't throw himself over backwards and hurt himself.

The roan fought back, pulling as hard as he could, but the line and halter were both strong enough to hold his weight, and all he did was hurt his neck.

As Cappy left him tied to the post and patted his quivering neck, the roan tried a quick two-legged kick at him. When the chain hit his hock and knee, he snorted and decided to stand still.

Cappy climbed out of the corral and went to the horse trough, where he bent over and washed off his peach fuzz face. He felt good. Standing by the water trough, he thought he'd done just like old Lou had showed him, and when they came back the kicker would be broke from that bad habit and he'd be halter broke besides. Another couple days and he'd be a fair rider, and if he was smart enough, he'd learn how to cut out a cow from a herd and set back and slide when his rider lassoed a critter, whether it be a calf or coyote.

Cappy probably wouldn't have run even if he'd had the chance, as half a dozen riders came at the barn and corral from all sides with their guns at the ready.

"It's the Askey kid," Roy Abbott said as the six men gathered about. "What are you doing here?"

"I work here." The boy was afraid, but standing straight.

"Even though that skunk of a Cromwell killed your dad?" Charlie Damker growled.

"I don't think he did that."

"What would you know about it?" Oakley Hunter asked.

"I know Dave Cromwell's been four square with me."

"Yeah? What's he paying you?" Phil Meredith sneered.

"I'm gettin' what every other cowhand gets, even if I ain't worth it yet."

"Where is he?"

"I don't rightly know."

"Don't get smart, kid, there's been too many men killed lately," Marshal Gus Fallon said bleakly, stepping down from his big, rangy skewbald. "I'm the marshal, understand? I represent the law. I want to talk to Cromwell and Wolford. Now, where are they?"

"It don't look like a law party to me. More's likely you got lynch on your mind," the boy said, close to trembling, but not backing up.

"You want to go to jail?" Gus demanded.

"I wouldn't tell you if I knowed."

*Splat!* The marshal's backhand knocked the boy sidewise to his knees.

"Get up!" Fallon yelled.

Cappy slowly got to his feet, his eyes not only unafraid, but now filled with pure hatred.

"Six on one ain't hardly fair," he said clearly, but the men ignored it. So anxious were they to get at Dave Cromwell they forgot they were grown men with guns beating up on a kid.

"None of your sass, kid. Where is he?"

"Why do you want him?"

*Whap!* went the open hand again, and the boy rose, this time with a trickle of blood leaking from the side of his mouth.

"If you find him, he'll kill you."

*Whap!* came the hand again. This time blood dripped from Cappy's left nostril.

"Where is he?"

"I do hope you find him. You'll all be wolf bait."

*Whap!* The boy went down again, his left eye swelling shut.

None of the riders made a move to stop the beating.

"Tell us!"

Cappy was thinking he couldn't hold out much longer. Pretty soon he'd be so mad and crazy he'd pop off and say the wrong thing. He was dizzy and spitting blood.

*Whap!*

"All right, Marshal," he gasped, "try the Flint Hills. Our place."

"You're lyin'!"

*Whap!*

He couldn't take any more of it, and he couldn't fight all of them.

Suddenly he dodged through the rail and

staggered into the corral, meaning to cut on across and run out the other side, but they were mounted and they quickly were spaced around the corral so that he'd made his own jail.

On the other hand, the marshal wasn't beating on him anymore.

"Stir up them horses," Roy Abbott said and snapped the nearest mustang with his quirt, sending him kiting around the corral mindlessly. The others started popping their lass ropes at the whirling, panicked mustangs so that no matter which way the boy ran, there was another one ready to knock him down. Dodging as best he could, Cappy tried to see all ways at once as the mustangs snorted and bucked and ran back and forth in all directions, their eyes wide in terror. The men on horseback, punishing the mustangs, were laughing and the marshal yelled, "You can come out when you want to tell the truth!"

"That's the truth!" Cappy yelled frantically as a blood bay hit him with his shoulder, spinning him against the sweating barrel of another.

"Tell us, damn you!" Fallon yelled.

But already he was down on hands and knees, his new boots scuffed and his new jeans dirty. A short-barreled calico knocked his hat off and skinned his forehead with a flying hoof. He rolled to one side towards the snubbing post, feeling as if he needed to throw up.

There was no way out and no place to go in this maelstrom of crazed animals.

The roan still haltered to the snubbing post was the only horse in the corral that wasn't crazy. He'd learned the halter, and he was afraid, but he wasn't kicking or bucking, and Cappy, in a last act of desperation, crawled close to the roan's feet, out of harm's way.

The roan might have kicked, but he knew it would hurt him, and he kept his feet bunched. As the swirling horse herd pressed against him he stepped sidewise so that Cappy was crouched under his belly. Still he didn't kick. He couldn't strike with his forefeet and he knew not to kick with his hind legs, so he stood there, trembling like an aspen leaf in a breeze.

"Get him out of there!" Roy Abbott yelled.

"Go ahead, Roy," Charlie Damker retorted, his face full of hate for the big-bellied man.

None of them were true horsemen. Most of them were afraid of their own mounts, so used to town life they'd become. None of them wanted to go into the midst of a bunch of crazy, wild horses.

"I'll get him out," Gus Fallon growled, pulled his Colt, aimed carefully, and shot the roan through the head.

The pony fell on his knees as if all its tendons and joints had been cut instantly; a hard front hoof smacked Cappy on the back of the head, then his bulk pinned Cappy to the ground.

"Goddamnit!" Roy Abbott yelled in frustration.

No one said "Let's go in and pull him free." There was no mercy in them, only fear.

The shot excited the mustangs all the more, and they slopped sweat off their shoulders and flanks as they dodged this way and that trying to escape or hide.

The riders gathered when the marshal mounted his skewbald.

"The Flint Hills ranch — anybody know it?" Fallon growled, enraged that a skinny kid could beat him.

"Sure," Charlie Damker said. "Wayne's family scratched a raggedy-assed livin' out there."

"Lead on," Fallon growled, thinking he'd like to shoot every one of these fat, rotten bastards just so he could breathe clean air again.

"Northwest about twelve miles maybe," Charlie Damker said, thinking he'd got to get Roy Abbott off by himself where he could shoot him. He knew it wasn't Cromwell strangling them, it had to be Abbott. Ambitious, Abbott wanted to own the whole town, the whole big pasture, and the railroad he came in on. So he was killing off everybody in town.

Charlie Damker didn't try to argue it out with himself, once he'd hit on it. He knew he was right and nothing could change his mind. By now, though, he'd learned from the night in jail that you had to play the cards quiet-like and look harmless, otherwise they'd say you were drunk or crazy and lock you up.

Now, as he remembered that night on the railroad bridge, he'd been against it all the time. He had tried to talk sense and nobody even listened, because Abbott was pushing all the time.

*I tried to save all those jaspers,* he thought. *I should have shot Abbott right then and set them boys free, but there was too many against me. Now Abbott wants my shop and my house, and he ain't agonna take 'em. Thinks he's the big he-boar in this town, but he ain't goin' to be nothin' when I finish with him.*

Leading the riders across the prairie toward the distant hills, Charlie Damker racked his brain to think of an easy way to gun Roy Abbott down, but as long as Abbott kept himself shielded by the other men, he didn't have a chance.

He'd have to wait. Darktime would be better.

An hour after Abbott and his crew had ridden away, a docile, hardworking team of four good horses came pulling a wagon-load of milled lumber. Old Lou sat contentedly on the seat, smoking his pipe, pleased that the heavily built mustangs had responded so well. Close by, Dave rode Coalie, working him through various gaits and leads to pass the time.

"Told you he was smart," old Lou said.

"He's more'n smart, he likes to work. Nothin' lazy about him. Just walkin', he gets worried as a duck in the desert, 'cause he wants to be doin' things."

They let the horses drink at the Bullfoot when they crossed, and Dave said, "I'll ride on in and get a fire started."

"Likely the boy'll have chuck ready," Lou smiled, "but go on."

At an easy lope, Dave rode towards the ranch, passed by bunches of Circle C stock, noting details of their looks, filing them away in the back of his head; and coming around the crest, he felt a small sense of relief that the barn was still there and the horses still in the corral.

In vain he looked for signs of Cappy, and thought the boy might be over by the creek, washing up, or maybe riding out a green colt.

He saw the signs of heavy horse traffic around the barn and alertly came around to the corral, where the mustangs were standing together in a single group, their heads drooping tiredly.

And there at the snubbing post crouched a dead roan, one he'd captured just last week.

Under the body of the horse he saw a hand extended out into the dirt and manure, and off to the left a stained and crumpled new Stetson.

Quickly dismounting, he crawled into the corral and saw Cappy's face poking out from under the horse.

He touched the boy's pale and bloody cheek and felt a warmth, heard the rattle of shallow breathing. He was alive!

What had happened?

Then he saw the bullet hole in the side of the pony's head and came to a quick conclusion. Riders had come to the ranch.

They'd run the boy through the wild horses and then dropped the roan on him.

As a killing rage roared hotly through his body, he made himself control it and get at freeing Cappy.

Which way to roll the horse? Want to keep the weight away from the boy's head.

The team halted by the barn, and old Lou came hustling in.

"He's alive," Dave said. "Think we can roll the horse off to his left?"

"We can." Lou dug his boot toes into the dirt and braced himself against the roan's hip. Dave took the front end, leaning on the withers.

"On three," Dave said. "One . . . two . . . three!"

They uncorked their knees and shoved, grunting hard as they moved.

The heavy-barreled animal shifted over under their pressure, then slowly toppled to its side.

Checking Cappy's shoulders, Dave decided they weren't broken and carefully pulled the boy loose from under the left hind leg of the roan. Once clear, Dave waited a moment, then gently rolled him over on his back.

"He ain't too busted up bonewise," old Lou said. "Question is, how he is inside?"

"I don't want to move him just yet," Dave said.

Cappy's eyes opened and stared at the sky a moment, then looked about.

"Cappy, it's Lou and Dave. Where does it hurt?"

Through mashed lips the boy said, "All over."

"You feel any bone ends grating? Cramp in your belly? Anything like that?" Lou asked. "Try movin' your legs."

Cappy bent one knee and then the other.

"That's a relief," Dave said, trying to joke, "you can at least walk to the outhouse."

"Move your arms now," Lou said.

The right arm lifted, then the left.

"My chest —" Cappy whispered, still staring at the sky as if confused and worried about some mysterious hostile creature up there.

"Sprung a couple ribs, likely," old Lou nodded to Dave. "He's young enough, he just bends, he don't break."

"All right, Cappy, we're goin' to rise you up and help you into the barn, where you can rest easy."

"You can holler all you want," Lou advised.

As gently as possible they lifted Cappy to

his feet, one under each shoulder. He groaned through clenched teeth. They walked him through the door into the barn and laid him down on a bed of hay.

Dave went for a basin of water and a washrag while Lou brushed the dirt and manure off the boy's clothing, murmuring, "You're goin' be all right now. Shouldn't have left you alone like that. My fault, I should have known. . . ."

"Nobody's fault," Cappy whispered. "The roan dead?"

"Head shot," Lou nodded.

"Darn —" Tears welled from Cappy's eyes. "So smart — had him all straightened out, ready to ride —"

Dave returned and cleaned the cuts on Cappy's face and learned what caused them.

"That marshal's a hard man," Cappy summed up. "Hope he don't hurt my ma."

"No reason to," Dave said. "They'll be ridin' back here as soon as they find out you set 'em on a false trail."

"And we'll be ready," old Lou said firmly.

# 9

The six riders of varied ages, backgrounds, and dreams were thinking in different ways about the simple problem of how to scrub the slate clean.

Oakley Hunter, being a newspaperman, had enough education to know that killing Dave Cromwell couldn't expunge the moral guilt they all had contracted that fearsome, fevered night on the bridge.

Roy Abbott, as the righteous son of a righteous abolitionist, had lived most of his life in Lawrence, and though educated only in merchandising, he understood there could be some crime possibly in the hanging of the four men without due process of law, but not guilt. He believed he'd acted according to the code of righteousness like a responsible citizen should, and therefore his conscience was clear.

Tom Fancher had funeralized so many men, starting in the Civil War at Chickamauga, so many he couldn't count, that he could not see that any moral value was important. You live, you die, and guilt is something made up by preachers and politicians. Indeed, he valued his own skin, because he liked the simple pleasures of life. Fine food, drink, and passionate women were body and soul to him.

Phil Meredith, the banker, was of the same opinion, except that he wanted more than the sensual pleasures — he wanted respect and admiration. He believed the way to gain a community's respect was to have the most money. Where that money came from wasn't important so long as the illusion was created that it was earned honestly. If he robbed a widow woman of her farm, it was important to stress that business was business, and if someone lost, someone else won, and commerce was the backbone of Western civilization.

Gus Fallon wasn't worried about the lynching. He hadn't been there, and he didn't think about it one way or another. He saw it only as a means to get a leg up in a world where aging gunfighters were scarce as bird shit in a cuckoo clock.

Charlie Damker, wheelwright and carpenter, had another slant on life in general and his own in particular. He didn't like bosses. He didn't want to be a boss, he just wanted to live by the honest skill of his trade. When he built a coffin, it was as well-made as the buyer could afford. If the grieving widow wanted a mortised and tenoned walnut box with four hinges on the lid and brass handles, he'd build it right. If the poor-mouth town wanted a pine box for a dead pauper, he'd nail the boards together solid enough to go under-ground without splitting.

He'd lived his life being independent. The money he earned was enough to keep him that way. He hired no helpers by the month, and neither would he take a monthly wage or orders from an overlord.

To him, good work was the moral to live by. After that, he was his own man and no-body better start telling him what to do or how to do it.

That's how it had started. When Roy Abbott started bossing him around like Abbott was the slave master and he was the slave, he resented it more than Abbott or anyone else knew. Maybe he was short and small, and maybe he'd come from no-where, but he was still his own man, and Roy Abbott had better learn that. Yet he hadn't objected at the bridge when Abbott was being the big boss, hadn't popped off his secret anger, so that it stayed inside, grew, and changed into a black devil of smouldering hatred that slowly ate into his common sanity.

What made Abbott think he was better than anybody else?

He was just a barrel of guts with a big mouth, that's all.

He couldn't read a rafter square or hang a plumb bob. He couldn't drive a cut nail nor saw to a line. He couldn't dowel or peg nor fit the simplest dovetail or shave a spoke. What the hell could he do?

He could buy cheap and sell dear to people who had no other place to go. How much brains did that take? So how does he come off saying do this and do that to a master wheelwright?

*Not this man. This man don't need to take any of the dictates of a hog like that nor anyone like him. He raw me much more I'm going set him right down on his big butt.*

It was this hatred that ate a layer of reason away from Charlie Damker's sensibility, releasing another demon which had been fearfully fermenting and growing in a parallel fashion ever since the hangings at the bridge.

He had helped to murder four independent men who had never bothered him in any way. They rode their own trails same as him, and he'd helped to take away their independent self-reliant lives.

He didn't know now how he'd gotten himself into it. Somehow the common excitement and all that puffed-up righteousness of Roy Abbott had drawn him into that group even though all his life he had never joined any club or lodge or tribe or clique or anything.

Sure he was sorry for the four dead men, but they were done and gone. What he wanted to do now was erase his error, clean off the stain, and regain his manhood.

This double hatred might still have burned him up inside slowly without ever erupting into open vengeance. He might have lived the rest of his life sullenly, going more sour every year, hating without speaking his hatred, wishing without taking revenge, but the effect of six killings of the strangler's committee created a seam in his soul for the volcano to blow off its pressure and erupt in fire and thunder.

He could read the plan of the avenger the same way he could read the plan for a dormer window. He could see how one by one they were being systematically eliminated, and he was afraid he was next.

Trying to think of a way to save himself, Charlie Damker came upon the idea that Roy Abbott had been the cause of the problem. If he'd give the avenging angel the body of Roy Abbott as a token of atonement, he would be released from the plan.

By killing Roy Abbott he would not only show the fat hog he couldn't order an independent man around, he would also pay him off for tolling him into a bunch of executioners, and even more important, he would give Roy Abbott's life to the avenger as full payment for his own.

So the mind of Charlie Damker constructed little boxes to fit inside larger boxes until he was completely sure of himself.

He'd fallen apart in the street when he'd seen himself reflected in the gaping grin on George Philbrick's dead face; he had lost his head and almost given himself away, but now he had control and carried a gun.

Seeing Roy Abbott giving commands to the boy and then running him down in the mess of wild horses only served to harden Charlie Damker's heart and make him all the more clever.

He meant to kill Roy Abbott as soon as possible.

It meant he'd have to get around Gus Fallon, who was nothing more than a bodyguard for Abbott, and that wouldn't be easy. Fallon was a master craftsman in his own way. He kept his tools clean and oiled. He bought the finest grade of powder and molded his own lead.

He wasn't after Fallon. Fallon had nothing to do with the work of the strangler's committee. He was only a bodyguard to a fool. Once Roy Abbott was dead, he'd go off to another job without thought of reprisal.

What Charlie Damker didn't take into account was his odd behavior. He was not a poker player, he was only a dour man of few words known to carry a chip on his shoulder and be some snorty when you forgot to say please. He had never thought to mask his feelings and never took into account that his gestures and facial expressions were as clear to an enemy as a two-page declaration of war.

His eyes glared sometimes wildly at Abbott's back as they rode, his mouth worked and leaked at the corners, his hands clenched and unclenched, and even the hunch of his thin shoulders seemed to be like an arrow aimed at Abbott's heart.

Roy Abbott was too absorbed in his own dream to pay any mind to the disintegration of Charlie Damker, but Gus Fallon stayed alive by reading much more subtle signs than these, and he was alert and ready for anything.

They rode in two files, Roy Abbott leading the left, Charlie Damker leading the right. Gus Fallon stayed to the rear, apparently to make sure they weren't followed, but he spent more time watching Charlie Damker than the back trail.

The others, not being natural riders, especially Phil Meredith, bounced around their saddles and drifted off the trail as their horses learned that their riders had no sense of horsemanship, only the ability to sit in a high-pommeled saddle and hang on to a high saddlehorn.

"You sure you know the way?" Roy Abbott yelled at Charlie Damker.

"Hell, yes. Your big butt sore?" Charlie yelled back.

"Watch your mouth, Damker."

"You don't want to follow my lead, you can go on back to your goddamned buttons and bows."

"What's got into you, Charlie?" Abbott demanded.

"Nothing." Charlie spurred ahead, inflamed with hatred and thinking, well, I sure told him off.

*Thinks I don't know the way out to Askey's. Sonofabitch never been out of the town. Ain't never seen the elephant or met the he-bear. I bet his ass is chapped with blisters and I hope they're bustin' out right now.*

*He just better watch it or he'll be smellin' brimstone before dark.*

Gradually they left the prairie and ascended low hills that became rockier as they ascended with a mixture of slate, chert, and flint. It was not as hospitable as the big pasture, but there was a beauty in the rolling hills, a difference of dimension that allowed the eye to roam instead of fix on an endless flat world all the way to a flat horizon. At least the hills had some relief even if the grass tailed off and the streams dwindled away.

When Charlie cut the trail he knew would lead into the Bullseye Ranch, he pulled up his sweating horse and turned to Roy Abbott.

"There it is," he pointed to the rutted trail. "Think I didn't know? Think you're so damned smart? Just ride on up them tracks, they'll take you right into the ranch. Or do you want me to lead you by the hand," he cackled wildly. "Poor Roy Abbott, he don't know beans from bullshit."

"Shut your rotten mouth, Damker!" Abbott bellowed, spurring his big horse against Charlie's crowbait. "Shut it or —"

"Or what?" Charlie asked. "You got us all into this. You ready to pay?"

"Pay? Pay? What the hell are you talking about!" Roy Abbott roared in anger and frustration, unable to comprehend what the wizened-up little carpenter was saying or wanted.

"You never pay. That's what I'm talkin' about. Take and take, that's your way."

"Settle down, Charlie." Gus Fallon rode in close. "Tighten your cinch, or you're goin' to take a fall."

"Just so everybody understands," Charlie said more calmly.

"Understands what?" Roy Abbott demanded. "What kind of a bee you got up your ass, Damker?"

"I think you know. You know how you tolled us into hangin' those boys for your own profit. Sure, you know. You just don't like to come out in the daylight and say so."

"I don't know what you're talking about."

"Forget it, then," Charlie Damker said. "Just foller them ruts over and catch your man."

Gus Fallon knew it all, because this was his line of business. He knew for sure that Charlie Damker had a hate on him that wouldn't let go, knew that in some devious way, Charlie Damker meant to kill Roy Abbott.

For his own part, he had only to weigh which man was the more valuable to him.

Fallon considered whether Roy Abbott would cut him out as soon as the town became safe again. Yes, sure he would. Abbott was a merchant. He didn't think of people as people, he thought of them only as potential customers. He would toss out the marshal whenever he thought his skin was safe. Yet, dead, he would be worthless. Eloise was the key to it. Dead, he wouldn't push on Eloise to accept him. Alive, he would play the game, thinking he could shut it down whenever he felt like it. But that way, Gus could possibly step in, marry his daughter, then be in the driver's seat. He could then kill him or let him live, whichever was more useful. So in order to win Eloise, her father did have considerable value to Gus Fallon.

Charlie Damker? What value was there in that chuckleheaded wood butcher? To Gus Fallon, nothing. Charlie Damker was a total loss as far as Gus was concerned. After he'd decided that, his mind was easy. He knew what was going to happen unless the luck went bad.

"You think they're at the ranch?" Abbott

199

asked Oakley Hunter as they rode ahead with Charlie Damker dropping back behind.

"There's no fresh tracks," Hunter replied, "but we've come this far, we might as well take a look."

Just ahead of Gus Fallon, Charlie Damker chuckled to himself. *Told the sonofabitch. Told him good. Nobody top dogs Charlie. Remember that? Never has, never will.*

*Now then, Dave Cromwell or whoever you are, I'm goin' to give you a present. Call it an offering, like exchanging gifts and smoking the peace pipe. I'm going to give you the polecat that thought up the lynching and you can lay off killing the rest of us, especially me.*

Spurring his horse, he came up close behind Roy Abbott and pulled his Colt. Aiming at his back, he paused a moment to think about who was really top dog when Gus Fallon shot him through the back and blew out his heart.

— *This'll teach you some respect . . .*

He never finished the thought. Dizzying spasms of glare and dark took over his mind as he fell dead, and Gus Fallon laughed.

They quickly drew up and Roy Abbott saw the sprawled body, the six-gun close by, and Gus Fallon with a tendril of

200

smoke curling out the barrel of his Remington .44.

"What!"

"Meant to backshoot you." Gus holstered the revolver. "Damn near did."

"But why?" Roy Abbott asked in amazement. "Me? Why me?"

"Loco," Gus said. "He's been gettin' squirrely for the past week."

"I knew he was mad about something, but not so mad he'd try to —"

"No great loss," Phil Meredith said disgustedly.

"I want to thank you, Gus, for saving my life," Roy Abbott said reluctantly, as if he didn't want to voice the debt.

"I'll probably ask you a return favor sometime," Gus Fallon smiled.

"By all means." Roy Abbott shuddered with fear and loathing for the man he knew was more clever than he'd thought.

Tom Fancher and Gus loaded the body onto Damker's horse and tied him on with his own rope.

"Damker must have planned this whole wild goose chase just to get a shot at my back," Roy Abbott said. "There's no sign at all of Cromwell or Wolford."

"And we're getting short of daylight," Phil Meredith said, wanting nothing more than to get back to the stuffed horsehide chair in his office.

The death of Damker took the fervor of the chase out of them. Now they were down to five members of a posse in which only Gus Fallon could be called a competent outdoorsman.

"We are off our home range," Oakley Hunter said, meaning that out here their five would mean little against Dave Cromwell and old man Wolford. They were putting themselves into a trap out here, whereas in town, it was the other way.

"Back to Ellsworth," Roy Abbott said firmly. "The kid lied."

From the window of the school, Eloise saw the group return. Her heart sank as she saw the body draped over the saddle, thinking they'd killed Dave. But Dave would never ride such a ratty horse, even in death. Then she recognized the paint-speckled dungarees of the carpenter.

Poor Charlie Damker, she thought. Still, what a relief to know it wasn't Dave.

Her heart seemed to lift and sing as she comprehended that her father had failed in his pursuit, and Dave was still alive and well.

Taking her leather briefcase full of test papers, she went out the door and locked it behind her, meaning to walk home and finish her grading of the tests there, but waiting for her on the street were her father and Gus Fallon.

"Hello," she said suspiciously, "what happened?"

"Damker tried to shoot me in the back," her father said sternly, as if somehow it might be partly her fault. "But Gus managed to cut him down first."

"I'm glad you're both all right," she said properly in the correct tone of voice.

"Once I had it figured out, he didn't have a chance," Gus Fallon said proudly and unthinking.

"You were . . . behind him?"

"He had your pa dead to rights," Fallon nodded with a smile, "but I made a fast enough draw to beat him."

"Congratulations," she said. "I'm going home now."

"Tell your mother to set an extra plate for Gus," Roy Abbott said.

"Yes, Daddy," she said again in that falsely proper tone. "I'm sorry I can't join you. I've a splitting headache."

With that, she turned away and walked swiftly down the street toward home.

"Sounds almost hostile," Gus Fallon growled meanly.

"You know how young ladies are," Roy Abbott said. "Scatterbrained as a grasshopper. Don't worry, she'll come along."

"The last thing I need is a bobcat in a briar patch," Gus said, forcing Roy Abbott into assessing his real worth to him. "I don't know how much you value your life, but it kind of wets down my powder when someone treats me like I was a gut wagon."

"I'll speak to her, Gus. Meanwhile, I'd like you to stay close until we turn up Cromwell."

"Like I said," Gus smiled, "I've no future here anymore. Dodge City is where the money is now."

"Gus," Roy Abbott said abruptly, making up his mind that the only thing between him and a wire around his neck was Gus Fallon, "I'll give you a square block of lots on Second Street if you'll stay and kill Cromwell."

"It ain't just the money, Mr. Abbott," Gus said, nailing down the lid. "I want to be respected. I want to have a wife and family and all that goes with it."

Roy Abbott said nothing. He considered how big an actual threat Dave Cromwell was, and he considered whether Gus Fallon would ever make a decent son-in-law, and he considered that his life's work had not yet been accomplished. He wasn't prepared to die just yet.

"Well?" Gus said.

"Well, I don't see why we can't make a family man out of you, son," Roy Abbott said, his pig eyes bulging as he screwed up a smile on his fat, puckered lips.

"That sudden headache?"

"I'm sure that's just temporary," Roy Abbott croaked as he read Gus Fallon's mean eyes and heard the iron in his voice. The thought occurred to him that he could use Eloise up until Cromwell was dead, then he could arrange for her to go to school back east, or if worse came to worse, he could arrange for an accident to happen to the big gunman dressed in black.

Tease the gunman along and get good value out of him. Then settle the debt.

Riding down First Street, the pair encountered Reverend P. G. Edenfield coming the other way, carrying his bible like a badge of office, as if by his simply packing the gospel around, people should listen to him speak and give him whatever he asked for.

"Afternoon, gentlemen," pink-faced Edenfield said piously. "I'm sorry to learn of brother Damker's demise."

"Why?" Gus Fallon had had a bellyful of false talk.

"Why, because he was a decent man . . ."

"He was a backshootin' loony," Gus said. "Get out of my way."

As the rosy-cheeked minister stepped aside, he said, "I still have hope for you, Mr. Fallon. Whenever you're ready to receive our Lord, please come see me."

At the Drover's Rest, Tom Fancher hurried to the bar and said gloomily, "Whiskey."

Tall, angular Tyson Tuck placed a sparkling-clean glass on the bar and poured the amber liquor to the brim.

"Doom," Fancher muttered as an habitual toast and tossed down the drink. "One more," he said, putting the glass back on the bar.

"Some fashed, ain't you?" Tuck offered mildly, pouring again. "This bourbon is the better for sippin'."

"Yes, and the better for clarifying a man's brain," Fancher said, weighted down with melancholy.

"Up to a point," smiled Tuck. "It's like tying a cow's tail to your bootstrap. It'll keep her from switchin' your face when you're milkin', but if she starts to run, you're goin' to spill the milk and bark your bottom."

Slender Luis Javier Fajardo merrily swung into a fast melody with his accordion, then, laughing, commenced a new song to the country.

> "Oh they say drink's a sin in Kansas
> They say drink's a sin in Kansas
> They say that drink's a sin
> So they guzzle all they kin
> And they throw it up agin
> In Kansas . . .
>
> Oh, they chaw tobacco thin in Kansas,
> They chaw tobacco thin in Kansas.
> They chaw tobacco thin
> And they spit it on their chin
> And they lap it up agin
> In Kansas!"

The house broke out of its dismal mood, and the customers at the bar quit listening to the doleful Tom Fancher and laughed and called for more.

"Go ahead, have your jokes," Fancher said blindly to no one. "There's only five left, and if I'm next . . ."

"Say now, that's a problem," Tuck laughed, "if you're next, who's goin' to bury you?"

"You can go to hell, all of you." Tom Fancher forgot his melancholy and angrily walked out the door with an air of dignified righteousness.

207

Going back over to the funeral parlor, he lighted a lamp and went to the table where Charlie Damker had been laid out.

He went through the pockets and found some coins, a sharp Barlow jack-knife, and half a plug of Star chewing tobacco. He removed the checkered tooled belt with its heavy brass buckle and then unceremoniously wrapped a length of cheap blue-striped ticking around the body and tied it securely with a piece of cotton sash cord.

Charlie hadn't thought to build his own coffin, and there was no one else in town who would do it.

"That's all you get, Charlie," Tom Fancher said, a little tiddley from the high-proof bourbon, "and that's all you deserve."

As he tied the last knot, he felt the cold wire come to his throat and bite down.

"What did you say up on the bridge, Tom?" a soft, pleasant voice drawled in his ear.

As he felt himself being lifted and laid on the table beside the body of Charlie Damker, he remembered the lurid scene and he remembered what he said — *"Let's get it done and over with"* — but he couldn't talk, and it was too late to try to explain.

# 10

Phil Meredith, spindle-legged and pot-bellied like a robin redbreast, paced the floor of the bank by the light of a single oil lamp. All of the profit from his life's work was housed in this solid brick building which he knew could not keep out the sinister strangler.

Nothing could stop him or head him off. There were only four of the original twelve left.

Why hadn't he left a note taunting the law, taunting the survivors, showing off how smart he was?

If they had a positive direct clue, they could call in a U.S. Marshal or fort up together or simply depart until he grew tired of waiting.

But there was always the doubt. He himself didn't believe Dave Cromwell could have handled all of them alone. Maybe by working some very fast moves with Lou Wolford, he might have been able to cover all that ground, but even that didn't add up. Wolford was just not the type of man to slip a length of wire around a man's throat, jerk it tight, and twist the ends together.

He swallowed and cocked his head nervously when he heard a mouse scurry in a dark corner.

It was just as possible, he thought, that one of their own was doing it. Damker might have been right, but after the wrong man.

After all, Gus Fallon was a killer and he hadn't been in on the hangings. Yet all of a sudden he became the marshal. Suppose the kid was a younger brother under another name?

A shiver ran down his spine because he knew that if it were Fallon, no one had a chance to elude him. He was too big, fast, and ruthless to stop.

Suppose . . . no, it couldn't be Roy Abbott. He was the ringleader. It was his goose. He'd have no reason to kill his own committee. And he wasn't physically strong enough to handle all the different men who had died by the wire.

Surely it wasn't P. G. Edenfield. Not unless he was completely insane. Suppose that's possible. No one kept an eye on his comings and goings. He was strong enough. Yet he appeared to be such a sweet, unctuous milksop.

Who else? Doc Faris? One-armed Pat Kimball, who ran the Hotel Ritz? The stranger named Hardisty? Another, maybe.

Hardisty and Tuck had come into town after the hangings. In fact, Tuck had taken up Malone's lease, and Malone had been the first to go. Yet what interest did they have in destroying the town? Hardisty had all the earmarks of a Texas cattleman. Tuck got his good whiskey from a brother in Tennessee.

Neither one of them looked to be clever enough to move like a cat in the night with a length of wire at the ready.

Besides, there were other newcomers climbing down off the train every day eager to settle down, and some were clearly on the run from something back east. Tuck and Hardisty — neither one of them was running. They never looked back over their shoulders. Tuck was always good for a good joke, and Hardisty just played solitaire all day, like he was waiting for the right piece of land to come his way.

Hardisty? Why not?

Yet they couldn't lynch them all just to get one madman.

From the distance he heard the mournful wail of a train chugging across the endless prairie, and he thought, *That's a signal to you. Say nothing. Pack up and go on the first fast train east.*

He really hated to abandon his pending deals, the blocks of lots he was ready to sell to the newcomers, the prairie land he'd filed on and meant to cut up into small farms. It was big. What a shame to miss out after he'd been so smart to be the early bird and had the patience to hold the land until the price went up.

Still, there was a fortune in the vault, more than he could spend in his lifetime.

*Take the morning train east to St. Louis. Change trains just to make sure nobody was following. Run up to Chicago, then straight east for New York. Put the money in Morgan's bank, then take a long vacation up in Maine.*

*Live like a gentleman instead of a nursemaid to a bunch of jayhawkers.*

A knocking at the door made him jump. He held his breath and waited.

The heavy knocking came again, then Gus Fallon's rasping voice, "Who's in there?"

Going to the door, but not opening it, the paunchy banker said, "Just me, Marshal."

"Anything wrong? I seen the light."

"Nothing wrong. Just working late."

"Afraid to open the door?" Fallon's laugh was a humiliation.

"Not exactly. I'm busy, is all."

"You're goin' to have to open it up in the morning," Gus Fallon chuckled, "or go out of business."

"I'd rather you were off finding the strangler instead of wasting my time with your stupid humor," Phil Meredith said, his voice rising high.

"Suit yourself."

He heard Fallon's boots thud away on the boardwalk with relief.

Whether Fallon was the strangler or not, he was still a raw, barbaric man who might do anything if his internal pressures blew up or if he saw something he wanted.

His own internal pressures were already too much. He could feel his heart pounding, his hands trembling. What was the good of it? *Get out and live the life of a leisurely gentleman while you can.*

His mind made up, he decided it would be unwise even to go over to the hotel to pack his clothes. First, he didn't want to give advance notice of his leaving, second, the strangler was out there, waiting.

He remembered the black horsehide sofa kept in the back room for occasional catnaps and decided he would sleep there.

*God,* he thought tiredly, *what good did it do to hang those four outlaws? It wasn't the hanging that had stopped the cowboys' wild-ness, it was Dodge City on west that was raking in the gold. If the drovers had a choice, they'd choose Dodge. So we hung them for nothing and we been paid back with double compound interest.*

Carrying the lamp to the back room, Phil Meredith unlocked the iron door imbedded in a brick wall, revealing tidy stacks of greenbacks and sacks of gold coins.

He felt like patting each stack of bills and stroking each bag of coins, but he also felt a need to hurry, and bringing out an innocuous-looking cowhide valise, he care-fully packed the money inside.

The gold made it heavy, even suspicious, he thought. If someone ever lifted it — but he would let no man touch it until he reached the safety of New York City.

Finished, he placed the bag inside the vault and relocked the iron door.

Blowing out the lamp, he told himself the first train eastbound would stop at six in the morning and he had to be there.

He must not oversleep.

Oakley Hunter — short, broad-shouldered, and ramrod straight — was also burning the midnight oil behind locked doors.

Sitting at his oversized desk mounded

with papers and books, he was holding his leonine head in his hands and squeezing his eyelids shut as if ready to receive a heaven-sent revelation. He waited, but he saw nothing except the four vague, indistinct forms topple one by one over the bridge, and what he heard was the creak of the tightening rope and popping neckbones.

"I don't want that," he said aloud, opening his eyes.

Before him was a piece of paper on which he'd been trying to clarify his thoughts. . . .

*Guilt? Most is Roy Abbott.*

*Least is me.*

*I spoke against it.*

That he really had not spoken against the hanging, he couldn't acknowledge now even to himself. By now his mind had per-suaded itself that he really had spoken forcefully against it.

*What to do?*

*Can't turn back the clock.*

*Can't bring back the dead.*

*Can find relatives and offer recompense.*

*Make a memorial, name streets for the dead.*

*Write a public apology.*

*Move out.*

*Blow up all Ellsworth and start over.*

"Oh, God —" he moaned into his hands

as he heard someone try the door.

"Who's in there?" came the raspy voice of Gus Fallon.

"It's me. I'm working. Don't bother," Oakley Hunter yelled back angrily.

"Just checkin'."

"Goodnight!"

From a curtained window in the parsonage built on the back of the First Four Square Church, a lamp cast its yellow glow which might have been interpreted by the faithful as a beacon of hope, but inside, a disordered mind was giving way to the devil.

The Reverend P. G. Edenfield was packing a steamer trunk. He was in no hurry. The westbound train would leave at seven o'clock.

In one section of the trunk he put his religious books, the Golden Hymn book, and his own notebook filled with sermons he had given and thought were worth giving again, especially in times when ideas were scarce.

Piling in most of his wardrobe, he closed the trunk and dragged it to the door.

His soft, cherubic face reflected a deep-seated joy as a dreamy smile played on his lips.

He had had a revelation! The first in his whole life. Nothing had moved him more, not even his first baptism in the south fork of the Red River. It had been such a profound experience, he felt as if he were floating gently in space, and his movements were lethargic and indecisive.

The lynching and subsequent stranglings had been preying on his mind, especially as it was his duty to console the widows and other survivors of those deceased. Fortunately there had not been so awful many of them, frontiersmen being somewhat shy of bringing their families into lands hardly vacated yet by the marauding Comanches.

He had come home to a lonely supper of corn soup and buttered biscuits brought over by the wife of Roy Abbott, whose devotion sustained him more than any of the other ladies in his parish.

Not to say it was all that bountiful. After all, he was an educated, cultured man of God, offering grace to all, and he was fed corn soup and biscuits while everyone else in town was eating fried beefsteak and potatoes and gravy.

He had eaten alone in the silent parsonage by the light of a lamp. In fact, he'd eaten it all, although he'd promised himself to deny his hunger.

It was after supper, as he sat in the big chair with the essays of Carl Adams Weatherill on his lap, that his eyes lost their focus, the room became hazy and grey, and he'd felt the heavenly angels lift him up into the evening sky, where he was ringed by flashing stars.

An angel had appeared before him saying, "Fear not, Phineas, for we bring good tidings."

P. G. Edenfield had almost nodded off into a drowsy lassitude, but he waited until another angel appeared. This one was a young man with broad, feathered white wings and a gleaming blue halo over his long hair.

"Phineas Elisha Edenfield, your work in Ellsworth is finished. You have proven to be a good servant. Now it is time for you to go forth into the wilderness preaching to the heathens and bringing them into the fold."

"Amen!" he'd cried out as he suddenly burst forth wide awake from the vision. "Thy will be done!" he added joyfully as if the weight of centuries had been lifted from his shoulders.

He would go forth into the wilderness where he could serve all the more. He would go to California and seek out those in need of salvation. He would immediately obey at all costs, even if it meant leaving his furniture behind.

It was then that he'd commenced packing. In the morning he'd tell Mrs. Abbott of his call and she could handle the problems of the church until another minister arrived.

The thought that he was running away from the scene of a crime never occurred to him, nor the idea that he was marked for death.

While these thoughts had obsessed him earlier, now he was aglow with the witness of revelation, and his mind was enchanted by his new mission.

He carried the lamp through the back door into the church and came around to face the simple altar, made of a table covered with a handmade cloth of fine linen. Behind the table on the wall was a cross made of two boards gilded to resemble gold.

On the table was a large bowl full of holy water, which served as a quick temporary baptism when the river was frozen over. To the right was a brass candelabra holding three candles.

Because of the importance of his revelation, he lighted the candles, then knelt before the table, facing the gilded cross, and commenced to pray.

"Our Father, who art in heaven . . ."

Over the low hill spiked with skewed crosses, the prairie wind rose and fell, singing its melancholy lamentation as it passed by through the night, and the color of a pink rose slowly came in the east as surely as God's promise.

The eastbound train stopped, but no passengers climbed aboard, and the train snorted and iron clashed as it pulled out.

An hour later the westbound train stopped, and a woman and her daughter — carrying a china doll — were helped up the iron steps by an impatient conductor who looked at his gold Hamilton watch and signaled for the engineer to move on out.

Ivan Jenkins, the bespectacled and balding teller of the First National Valley Bank, came up the brick steps and started to put his key in the brass-faced lock, but the door opened under the slight pressure, and puzzled, he cautiously stepped inside.

Nothing seemed to be disturbed, and he decided that Mr. Meredith had inadvertently left the door open when he went home. It wouldn't do. He'd have to mention it in a cautionary way.

Raising the slatted blinds, he let the sun in and then went to the back room for the broom.

There in the dim light he saw Phil Meredith sleeping on the horsehide settee. His hands were clasped over his pigeon breast. Over each eye lay a twenty-dollar gold piece.

*Let this be a lesson to all men . . .*

Ivan Jenkins squalled as if he had a shirt full of bees and ran for the marshal.

Virgil Patrick, a wandering typesetter addicted to the bottle, was late for work. He'd already had two drinks, but he still felt a throbbing in his head and a queasiness in his stomach. Yet he believed from past experience that his fingers would soon be flying across the boxes of type, putting the cast metal letters in the stick, line after line, paragraph after paragraph, with the help of an occasional nip, and the day would pass by in a pleasant haze. Then off to the Drover's Rest, where he could go beyond the plateau into blissful oblivion.

The paper was already made up and ready to print except for Oakley Hunter's editorial, which was always the last piece to come in.

He should be rolling the press by noon, and in a couple of hours the week's edition would be ready for distribution.

Virgil Patrick had lately begun to feel the pull of the road, even though he'd arrived in Ellsworth only four months earlier, riding a freight.

The town wasn't as peaceable as he'd hoped, and it seemed to have gone from bad to worse. *There must be better places,* he thought, and though he disliked riding the cars, he did like to see the country.

Surprisingly, Oakley Hunter wasn't at his desk, yet the door was wide open.

*Probably gone across the street for coffee,* Patrick thought and went to the back of the printshop for his ink-stained canvas apron.

Passing the press, he immediately noticed that the editorial page had already been set and locked on the press. Not bothering to read the type, he continued on to the storeroom, where he kept his apron and spare bottle.

Opening the storeroom door, he was met by the body of Oakley Hunter — a wire around his neck and hanging from the brass hook where his apron ought to be.

Upon his vest was pinned a proof page of newsprint.

From his black, swollen face, Oakley Hunter's eyes bulged out, staring into eternity as if he'd seen his future and it was a horror.

*I don't know . . .*

In a split second Virgil Patrick had turned and scuttled out the front door, yelling for the marshal.


Mrs. Roy Abbott wrapped a half a pan of cinnamon rolls in old newspaper and set off for the parsonage on her daily mission of charity and goodwill.

It wasn't so much that she feared P. G. Edenfield would starve to death, but she rather enjoyed a few minutes in his company. He made her feel young and desirable again, although he never so much as patted her hand solicitously. It was that he was a younger person with some education and culture. He had attended Chautauqua meetings, where all the great ideas were discussed and the latest in plays and other moral entertainments were presented.

And his eyes were big and brown and moist as a puppydog's.

He appreciated her cooking too, always smiling and saying how tasty this was, how felicitous the pie, how zestful the cookies, sometimes kissing the tips of his fingers and rolling up his beautiful, enchanting eyes.

Knocking at the parsonage door, she waited. *He should be home preparing the sermon for tonight's prayer meeting,* she thought, vexed to think she'd miss her morning visit if he'd been called away suddenly. Rapping again, she waited, then wondered what to do with the cinnamon rolls.

After one more knock on the door, she turned the latch and went inside.

"Reverend . . ." she called, and saw the steamer trunk packed for travel.

Placing the rolls on the round dining table, she stood quietly and listened.

Nothing. *Such a serenity,* she thought, wishing her own home could be that way.

Possibly he was in the church.

Calling again, "Reverend . . ." she proceeded through the door and walked softly around to the front of the altar.

There she found him, bowed over his prayer rail, arms dangling limply, his clothes sopping wet from the big, salt-glazed bowl that had been dumped over him. Then she saw the twisted ends of the wire protruding from the back of his neck.

*Repent your sins!*

Her screams were loud enough to be heard at the other end of town, and then mercifully she fainted.

Marshal Gus Fallon admitted Roy Abbott into the back room of the bank, where Ivan Jenkins waited, miserably contemplating his future.

Nothing had been disturbed. Phil Meredith lay as before, a sleeping man with shining golden eyes.

"Good Lord!" Roy Abbott said as he viewed the remains.

"Where were you last night?" Gus Fallon glared at Jenkins.

"I was home in Ma Dove's rooming house all night," he said defensively.

"Can you prove it?"

"Certainly. Mr. Tuck was there. I met him in the hall. He can vouch for me."

"You liar!" Gus Fallon leaped at the little man and slapped him with his open hand.

"Easy — slow down, Marshal," Roy Abbott said sharply. "We've got to work this out."

"It's simple. This scum figured to take over the bank if he could get rid of Meredith. He had the key to the front door, he knew Meredith would be sound asleep, and he could blame it on the strangler."

"It's all right, except Jenkins hasn't got the guts," Roy Abbott said strongly. "No, it had to be Cromwell. Who else?"

"I sure as hell wish I knew," Gus Fallon said bitterly. "I'd hang him high."

"Cromwell," Roy Abbott said decisively. "There's no one else."

"Look, Abbott, I can handle Cromwell, but I ain't goin' out to that ranch and try to fight him and old Wolford and a dumb kid and maybe some more he's brought in for protection."

"No, of course," Roy Abbott said. "We've got to get up a posse of the people. Call up the railroad workers. They haven't done anything. Find some drovers. If he sees a dozen riders well armed, he'll either give up or go to ground. Either way, we've got him."

Suddenly they heard the caterwauling of Virgil Patrick screeching from across the street.

"Boil me for a sea horse, by God, I'm goin' to tear somethin' loose!" raged Gus Fallon wildly as he ran toward the front of the bank, a six-gun in either hand.

There in the middle of the street was the slight and stooped Patrick baying at the empty sky, "Marshal! . . . Help! . . . Murder! . . . Marshal! . . ."

Instantly Gus Fallon fired two shots into the air, shutting off Patrick's howl and scattering the gathering crowd of towns-people.

"What the hell is it, you idiot fool of a hammerheaded jackass!" Fallon roared.

Patrick pointed abjectly to the open door of the printshop.

Gus Fallon charged across the street with both guns at the ready. Bursting through the door, he stopped and swept the long room with blazing eyes.

Jesus God Almighty, he wanted to kill somebody so bad, he could almost taste it.

Then in the empty room he saw the slumped figure hanging from a closet hook in the back.

Roy Abbott came up close behind him. Holstering his guns, Fallon untwisted the wires, letting the body crumple to the floor, while Abbott removed the proof sheet from the vest.

"What do you make of it?" Abbott asked.

"I make it that Cromwell has done cut loose his wolf!" Tight-lipped, Gus Fallon shifted his eyes around, looking for a surprise attack.

Going to the front of the shop where there was better light, Roy Abbott read from the proof sheet aloud, even as Eloise entered, followed by Tyson Tuck, old Doc Faris, Pat Kimball, and Alvin Hardisty.

"Editorial — The citizens of Ellsworth, Kansas have had enough. They want peace and tranquillity in their homes. They want to hear the sound of commerce thriving in the business district.

They want to welcome new settlers with open arms and a promise of a decent future in the rich Smoky Hill Valley.

They can do none of these things while a man roams the streets in the night murdering defenseless (sic) citizens.

Let us admit that this man might have some just cause. Four men who had not been convicted of any crime by a legally sworn jury before a circuit court judge were hanged recently without a trial.

Justifying this action was the horde of cowboys running wild in the street, out of control, giving our city a bad name. Compounding this was the tragic death of a child, which precipitated a call for instant relief.

Now, looking back, the writer acknowledges that hanging was too severe a punishment for whatever illegal acts these men committed.

Therefore, I say to the nameless man or men who stalk the dark streets of our city, we apologize. We cry to our God for mercy. We beg forgiveness from anyone who seeks revenge.

Vengeance is not the proper answer, for vengeance begets even more violence.

Let the writer say in conclusion, that I myself am most profoundly sorry that I forgot wisdom and fell victim to passion that sorry night, and that I offer whatever I have to recompense the families of these men, and offer the rest of my life in atonement. . . ."

Penciled in block letters across the bottom of the page were the words: THANK YOU.

"The devil —" muttered Gus Fallon, "I want a posse to go out there and get Cromwell."

"That may not be necessary," Hardisty said.

"Who are you to say anything?" Fallon turned to face Hardisty, ready to draw.

Before Hardisty could reply, the animal's

229

scream tearing from the throat of Mrs. Roy Abbott shattered the tense moment.

"What . . . ?" Gus Fallon turned side-wise, listening.

"That's mama!" Eloise cried out.

"The church!" someone outside yelled, and the crowd opened to clear a way for Gus Fallon, Roy Abbott, Alvin Hardisty, and Tyson Tuck.

Bursting through the front door of the church, they saw Abbott's wife staring up at the gilded cross, her arms upraised, howling like a dog in pain.

Roy Abbott reached her first, grabbed her, pinning her arms down to her sides and shouting, "I'm here!"

Gus Fallon and Alvin Hardisty were kneeling beside the dead preacher.

"Went to heaven freshly baptized," Tuck said.

Eloise took her sobbing mother from Roy Abbott and sat in the back pew, while only the boldest of the townsfolk dared enter the church to witness the grisly scene.

"That only leaves you," Gus Fallon said to Roy Abbott.

"Just because you missed the hanging, doesn't make you so snow white," Roy Abbott said defiantly. "You've been with us hand in glove ever since, and don't think he doesn't know it."

"By God, I'd give a hundred dollars if he'd step in here right now and face me fair," Gus Fallon roared.

"You know he won't," Roy Abbott snarled back. "We need to go out and get him. Get some real men together and just go bring him in."

"For a fair trial," Hardisty said quietly.

"Hell, yes, for a fair trial. About as fair as he gave Edenfield, or Hunter, or Meredith!" Abbott yelled.

"It won't do," Hardisty said coolly. "There'll be no more lynching in this town as long as I'm around."

"Just who the hell are you to be giving orders, mister?" Fallon boomed, enraged so much that froth came spitting out with his words.

"I'm a U.S. Marshal out of Topeka." Hardisty pulled a gold badge from his vest pocket. "And you're going to do what I say from now on."

"Well, why the hell didn't you say so?" Fallon growled. "I mighty near shot you."

"I wasn't worried, Fallon," Hardisty said levelly. "You're musclebound. It makes you slow."

# 11

Dave Cromwell walked beside a horse harnessed to a rock sled half filled with flat limestone slabs pried from the hillside by the creek. Coming to the cabin site, he stopped the horse and placed the rocks in a ditch alongside a tight cord.

Nearby, old Lou was troweling mortar between the joints of other rocks already in the foundation, while young Cappy stood off to one side, watching and learning.

Cappy's upper chest had been bound tightly with strips of an old sheet, nearly immobilizing him, but making sure his cracked ribs didn't move.

"I bet I can do something," he said to Dave.

"Couple more days, Cap. Take it easy while you can."

The foundation for the rectangular building was almost finished, and though the work would never pass a journeyman mason's standards, it would last longer than any frame building it would be called upon to hold up.

"Comes a twister, we want her anchored down good," Dave explained to Cappy. "Besides, the rocks help keep the bugs out."

"When are them hombres comin'?" Cappy asked, scanning the river road worriedly.

"They'll come soon enough, just like a goose goes to water," old Lou said.

"And we're as ready as we'll ever be," Dave smiled. "After all, there was only five of them."

"That cloud of dust I been watchin' looks less'n any five riders would make," Cappy said.

"I make it to be two," Dave said, looking off towards the road. "C'mon, you and Lou are goin' to move into the barn."

Quickly the three of them prepared for battle.

Lou and the boy took positions downstairs, Lou with his big scattergun and the boy with a Spencer repeating rifle, fully loaded.

Upstairs at the loft window, Dave had built a barricade of lumber, hay, kegs of nails, and horseshoes. Beside him was a .44-40 Winchester, and in his holsters were the two improved Remington six-shooters.

Early on he recognized Gus Fallon and the stranger in town, Alvin Hardisty. From his high lookout, he watched to make sure there were no others hiding out yonder.

Climbing down the ladder, he said, "Best stay here. I'll parley with 'em."

"We'll keep 'em covered, Dave," the old man said.

Dave, carrying the rifle in the crook of his arm, went outside to meet the two riders.

"Howdy," he said, facing the two riders.

"Looks like you're rebuilding," Hardisty said, seeing the foundation work.

"Some," Dave said. "How come you're ridin' with a skunk like him?"

"Now, Dave, take it easy," Hardisty said mildly.

"Who the hell are you callin' a skunk?" Gus Fallon had his hand on the butt of his revolver.

"I'm sayin' that boy you hammered on with your fist and run through a herd of wild ponies has a bead right on your brisket, mister."

Gus Fallon opened his hands and placed them carefully on his saddlehorn.

"That kid's a traitor to his pa," he said weakly, sweat beading his broad forehead.

"What do you want, Hardisty?" Dave asked bluntly.

"There were three people killed last night in town. I don't know if you did it or not, but under the authority of the U.S. Marshal's office, I'm taking you in for trial."

"You're crazy," Dave said shortly. "I was here all night."

"I'm not the judge. I'm just a U.S. Marshal sent to settle all this trouble. The judge will be in on the night train and hold court tomorrow."

"Then I'll come in and talk to him to-morrow."

"No, my duty is to have you there waiting," Hardisty said firmly.

"Look, Hardisty," Dave said, "I was marshal there in town once, and I saw what those nice people can do to helpless prisoners."

"I'll guarantee your safety."

"I told those boys in the cell I'd fight for them, but once I got knocked in the head, they didn't have a chance."

"Nobody's goin' to knock me in the head," Hardisty said, "and I'll keep an eye on Marshal Fallon too."

"I don't like it. I'm just a peaceable man tryin' to build up a ranch, why should I waste my time?"

"I'll tell you why," Hardisty said. "You

235

respect the law. That's it, plain and simple. You know you have to live by the rule of law, or you'll never have anything."

"Somethin' to that, but why me?"

"Because most of the town except me thinks you're the strangler, and I think once you're proved innocent, we can smoke out the real killer."

"All right," Dave said, "I'll go peaceable on the condition that I keep my guns."

"Not in the jail cell."

"You damned right, in the jail cell," Dave spoke hotly. "I'll be safe enough if I can defend myself."

"All right," Hardisty relented wisely, "you do have a right to defend yourself."

"All right." Dave faced the barn. "Lou, Cappy, I'm goin' in like he says. There'll be less chance of someone startin' trouble if you stay here."

"Hardisty," Lou called out, "I'm holdin' you responsible."

"I'm going to get this mess cleaned up while there's still a town left," Hardisty said. "The U.S. Attorney General don't hold with folks taking the law into their own hands."

"Watch Fallon, Dave," came the clear, high voice of Cappy. "He'll turn on you like a rattlesnake, you give him a chance."

Dave mounted Coalie, set the rifle in its scabbard. "Let's ride."

With Hardisty in the center, the three riders headed back toward town, and Lou and Cappy came from the barn.

"I sure hope he knows what he's doin'," Cappy said, worry wrinkles creasing his forehead.

"He's doin' right, but sometimes it ain't too healthy to volunteer like that," Lou said mournfully.

On the way to town, Gus Fallon said to Hardisty, winking broadly, "I been eatin' about every night over at Roy Abbott's house. His daughter just loves to cook for me."

"You better shut up, Fallon, before I let my prisoner kill you," Hardisty said tightly.

"Keep on talkin'," Dave said. "You sound just like a puffed-up bullfrog croakin' under the outhouse."

"You'll be singin' another song soon enough," Gus Fallon growled.

In the Drover's Rest, Tyson Tuck swabbed the long bar, which was nearly empty except for a sodden Virgil Patrick, a couple of drummers, a tinhorn easterner writing for the *Police Gazette* about the wild and wooly west, and the slim Mexican jack-of-all-trades, Luis Javier Fajardo, who was scattering fresh sawdust over the floor.

"Been out here a long time?" the reporter, a round, little man with sideburns and steel spectacles, asked Tuck.

"Not long," Tuck said.

"Do you plan to stay or move on west?"

"Depends," Tuck said awkwardly, looking down at the journalist.

"I understand there have been close to a dozen killings in Ellsworth in the past month."

"That's close, if you don't count the four that was lynched."

"How long do you expect this bloodbath to continue?" The reporter scanned his notes and scribbled more.

"I'd say another day or two," Tuck smiled, his long arms and big hands working on the bar. "Less'n you volunteer to stretch it out."

"Not me. I'm just the reporter. I try to find the truth and tell it as it is."

"Then if'n I was you, I'd go way back to early summer and learn all about those four that was fitted with hemp neckties."

"Know their names?"

"I don't suppose anyone remembers. You could find 'em on the headboards up on Smoky Hill."

"And where would that be?" The reporter got to his feet.

"Up at the corner turn right. Follow River Road south to where you see the railroad bridge. Just off to the left is Smoky Hill. Can't miss it."

"I saw it from the train when I come in. Did you know any of them?"

"Can't say I did." Tuck smiled again.

The reporter was trained to discern shades of the truth, and he felt an alarm bell ringing in the back of his head. Something wasn't right. Thinking about it, he realized Tuck had not really told him anything he didn't already know.

"Where do you come from, Mr. Tuck?" he asked casually, putting the note pad in his breast pocket.

"Beegum, Tennessee. Why?"

"You have a touch of the Kentucky accent in your speech." The reporter patted a golden sideburn.

"I must've got it from my ma. She's from Kentucky. Related to Abe Lincoln on the Hanks side."

"Big family?"

"About average. Five brothers and six sisters."

The reporter was suddenly afraid of something he couldn't believe. Looking up at the extra-tall gangling man with the cleft chin, tight round cheeks, and deep-set eyes, he decided to fade into the woodwork to wait and see.

"I've heard about those big Kentucky families. They take care of their own," he concluded, pushing his glass forward for a refill.

"Stayin' long?" Tuck asked conversationally.

"I can wait another day or two."

Stepping out of the Drover's Rest, the reporter mopped his face with his handkerchief. The mockery in those eyes! Behind that was a sense of ancient certitude that came in the blood, a sorrow — yes, a pity, perhaps — but the iron certitude overruling it all.

Reminded of Abraham Lincoln, he thought of the martyred president who had sent thousands and thousands of young men to die for the simple principle of maintaining the union. There had been in his eyes that same sense of sorrow being superseded by the sense of unyielding rightness.

Those Kentuckians!

In the glare of day the sense of enthrallment in mystery dissipated, he decided against going all that way to Smoky Hill.

Even as he considered whether to go talk to Roy Abbott or Pat Kimball at the Ritz, three riders turned the corner and came down the street.

A huge bear of a man on the left wore a brass star, the man on the right wore a soft grey shirt and a simple cowhide vest, and the man in the middle was a few years older and wore a U.S. Marshal's badge on his buckskin vest.

Here was the story unfolding right before his eyes.

He studied the men carefully as they rode on by and stopped at the jail. They were all armed, and they were definitely dangerous, as they seemed to rub sparks off each other.

The town marshal was named Gus Fallon, a gunfighter notorious along the border. The one in the middle had to be the former marshal, Dave Cromwell, that he'd heard so much about, and the U.S. Marshal was definitely a no-nonsense lawman who had taken control.

Hurrying along after them, he was at their heels as they entered and went on past the office down the short hall to the single cell.

He saw Dave Cromwell go into the cell, still wearing his two six-guns strapped to his thighs.

What a story!

241

As the door clanged shut and Hardisty turned the key, he came up close. "Name's Owensby, Neil Owensby. I write for the *Gazette*, and I'd like to interview the prisoner."

"He's not exactly a prisoner; he's volunteered to stay here until the judge comes," Hardisty said.

"He'd tell you nothin' but lies anyways," Gus Fallon said. "You want the truth, talk to me."

"I will later, Mr. Fallon, of course."

"There's nothin' much to tell," Dave said.

"C'mon, Fallon," Hardisty said firmly, "I'll be handling the jail for a while."

"How do you get that way?" Fallon protested.

"Easy. If I look hard enough I can find a bounty poster on you. I recollect something about a sporting girl killed down at Fort Brown on the border some years back —"

"It wasn't me," Fallon said quickly, "but hell, there's no sense arguin' about the damned jail. It's your play."

"That's for sure," Hardisty said. "Now go on and tell the folks the party's over. There ain't goin' to be no more killin'."

As Hardisty settled down at the desk in front to compose a telegram for headquarters in Topeka, Neil Owensby stood in the hall, talking to Dave.

"How many men attacked you when you were the marshal?"

"I guess only one hit me over the head, but there was a dozen of them took my prisoners."

"Did you recognize them?"

"They had sacks over their faces, but I knew them all."

"How did you feel when they executed your prisoners?"

"I was some unsociable," Dave said carefully.

"You were mad?"

"Of course. If I could have pushed the whole slough of 'em off that bridge, I sure would've."

"Do you still carry that grudge?"

"If you're tryin' to ask was I mad enough to run them down one by one and strangle them with a wire, the answer is no."

"Of course, you have an alibi."

"Most of the time my pardner was with me."

"An ambitious prosecuting attorney could tear that to pieces very quickly."

"I'm not worried."

"Do you feel any remorse for those that have been killed?"

"Only that they were all fired up by Roy Abbott and didn't realize the consequences. Otherwise, I figure they just paid up, that's all."

As Dave talked to the journalist, Gus Fallon waited in the back room of the Mercantile until Roy Abbott could finish with a customer.

Hurrying into the room, Abbott, barely under control, gritted his teeth and said, "Why didn't you kill him?"

"Mister, I don't kill nobody with a U.S. Marshal lookin' over my shoulder."

"Tell me the situation exactly," Abbott asked angrily, his jowls shaking like wattles on a tom turkey.

"He's locked in the cell, but he has two six-guns loaded. The judge will settle the whole shebang tomorrow. That's it."

"So Cromwell will get off because there's no hard evidence against him except the motive."

"Likely."

"That just is not going to happen. We've got to stir up the town and hang him high before morning."

"And what do I get out of this?"

"You know what you get," Roy Abbott said strongly, "but don't be a hog about it."

"But who has the final word?" Gus Fallon pressed the message home.

"You do," Roy Abbott said. "She's yours if Cromwell dies."

"I'll hold you to that," Fallon nodded.

Shortly afterward, Roy Abbott strolled into the Drover's Rest, put a stack of silver dollars on the bar and said, "Buy the house a drink."

The problem was that there weren't many customers in the Rest, and none of them looked like fighting men.

The drummers at the end of the bar saluted him as Tuck poured their drinks. Virgil Patrick was oblivious to the world but was still able to down one more drink. A couple of German immigrants, who didn't know a trigger from a hammer, and three cowboys, who had just come up from the Red Dog for a change of scene, were the only possibles.

Of the townspeople only one-armed Pat Kimball of the Hotel Ritz was present, and so far he'd stayed completely out of the trouble.

"What do you think, Pat?" Roy Abbott asked as if wanting advice and respecting Kimball's word.

"About what?" Kimball asked, feeling strange because Roy Abbott had never asked his opinion about anything before.

"That U.S. Marshal sneaking in under cover and then taking over our town."

"First I heard of it."

"Another round, Tuck." Abbott shoved a couple more silver dollars over. "Well, it's a helluva thing. Feds running our town when they don't know nothin' about it. After all, we're the ones that fought the Injuns and built our town with no help from the Feds."

"That's for sure," Pat Kimball nodded agreeably. "It's not been easy nor a free ride by a long shot."

"What do you reckon we ought to do?" Abbott asked again, man to man.

"Kick their butts out of town!"

"Whose butt we gonna kick out of town?" one of the cowboys asked, tossing off his whiskey.

"They's only one U.S. Marshal thinks he can run us. He's already taken over the jail. Next he'll be takin' this saloon, and my store, and then what'll we have?" Roy Abbott raised his voice as he orchestrated the men.

In a few minutes a subtle change came over the group. Even the drummers were volunteering for service against the Feds.

Abbott hoped that Gus Fallon was

having the same results in the Red Dog. A dozen angry citizens carried a helluva lot of authority, and he had a half a dozen right here in the palm of his hand.

Abbott continued to buy the drinks and slowly build the conversation into a slow-burning anger. Playing on the frustrations and fears of his audience, he gradually increased the pitch.

As soon as it was dark, he thought, he'd pull the string.

Down at the Red Dog, the rougher crowd of thirsty drovers was pleased to agree with the big, gunfighting town marshal that the Feds should keep their noses out of Ellsworth County and the state of Texas as well as Montana, Nebraska, and Wyoming.

"Drink up, boys, let's have another!"

Some of the noise from the Red Dog could be heard two doors down at the jail, and Alvin Hardisty added to his telegram, "Please send reinforcements immediately."

Neil Owensby, feeling pleased that he was garnering enough material to last him all winter if he dressed it up and exaggerated the truth somewhat, came down the hall, paused at the desk where Hardisty sat and said, "It's quite a mystery."

"I don't know about that. Are you going down to the telegraph office?"

"As a matter of fact, I'm heading that way right now to file a story."

"Take this along and have it run ahead of yours. I'm not taking any chances."

Owensby read the message quickly and whistled. "You think the vigilantes will try to break in the jail?"

"No, I just want to cover all the rat holes. Now, git."

As the journalist hurried out the door, he almost collided with Eloise Abbott, who was coming the other way.

"Pardon me, ma'am," he said, hurrying on.

"I heard Dave Cromwell was in here," she said, coming on into the office.

"Yes, ma'am, he is."

"What's he charged with?"

"Nothing," Hardisty said grimly. "Fact is, if someone gets murdered tonight, it will put him in the clear."

"There's only my father left. Why aren't you protecting him too?"

"Your father told me to mind my own business."

"May I see Dave?"

"I reckon he'd like that." The marshal led the way down the hall.

"Lady wants to talk with you, Dave."

"What's there to talk about?" Dave responded warily.

"Things are heatin' up in the Red Dog, Dave," Hardisty said, unlocking the barred door. "Just pretend that door is locked unless there comes more trouble than I can handle out front."

After Hardisty had gone back to the office, Eloise said, "I don't know what's happening, Dave."

"You know as much as me. Between your pa and Gus Fallon, you ought to have the whole story."

"Dave, I despise that man," Eloise said strongly. "If we can't settle all this trouble right soon, I'm leaving town."

"Where to?"

"As far away as I can go."

"But why?" Dave asked, shaken by the determination in her voice.

"That man Fallon has some kind of a hold on daddy, and I can't go along with it."

"What kind of a hold?"

"I don't know." Her lower lip trembled. "I guess it's because deep down daddy is scared to death."

"What's he scared of?"

"You," she said softly. "He thinks you're

the strangler, that you're just saving him for last because you hate him so much."

"It's true that I wouldn't spit on him if he was afire, but I just don't hold with an eye for an eye. If somebody wants to fight, I'll sure try whippin' him, but too many innocent people get hurt if you start feuding. Can you tell him that?"

"You don't know how stubborn he can be."

"Listen, Eloise," Dave said earnestly, "after tonight I'm goin' to find the strangler even if your dad won't admit the responsibility for lynching those men."

As the evening progressed, Roy Abbott had a brilliant idea bloom like a lightning bolt in his mind. The perfect solution! He examined the idea carefully from every angle and decided it couldn't miss.

"Give these boys anything they want," he said, shoving the remaining silver dollars across the bar. "I'll be back in a minute."

Hurrying down the boardwalk to his store, he let himself in, locked the door behind him, and lighted a lamp.

Raising the door to the basement stairway, he took the steps two at a time and, by the light of the lamp, found a keg of black powder, a blanket-padded canteen, and some blasting fuse.

Using a funnel, he poured the canteen full of powder, inserted a length of fuse, stoppered the canteen with a cork, then proceeded to wrap a cord over the fuse, tying it tightly to the canteen so that it couldn't be ripped out.

Making an innocent package of the bomb with a newspaper and wrapping string, he left the tip of the fuse exposed for lighting.

He hurried out the back door into the alley. The jail was just next door. The small, high window showed a weak lamplight, and he could faintly hear voices coming through the barred window.

Hiding the bomb under a packing crate, he went back through the store, out the front door, and across next door to the Red Dog Saloon.

"How's it going, Marshal?" Roy Abbott asked, heaving for breath.

"These boys want to have a talk with that Cromwell strangler fellow," Gus Fallon grinned, and there was a general drunken hue and cry from the pack of freeloaders Fallon had gathered.

"Fine. There's some others over at the Rest that want to join up too. Let me get them."

Trying to go slow so that he wouldn't be

breathing so hard, he made his way up the street to the Drover's Rest, where he hailed the few cowboys and the drummers who were worthless except for a show of numbers.

"Let's go!"

"I sure hope you know what you're doin'," Tuck said unsmiling, staring fixedly at Roy Abbott.

"Come along, Tuck, and I'll show you who runs this town, and for damned sure it isn't the Feds!"

Out they went into the street just in time to mingle with the group following Gus Fallon. One door down stood Hardisty with a double-barreled sawed-off shotgun cradled over his arm.

"Hold it right there!" Hardisty yelled, noting Roy Abbott slipping furtively into his store.

Even while Hardisty was holding back the drunken mob, Roy Abbott ran out the back door and recovered the bomb. Lighting it with a phosphor, he stood on the crate, lobbed it up through the window into the cell, and ran to the back door of the store again.

The bomb came through the window as Eloise was preparing to leave. Had Dave not seen the sparks spitting from the package, he might have lost it all right then, but the image he saw was translated instantly into action.

"Run, Eloise!" he yelled, and knowing he couldn't throw the bomb out the small barred window, he kicked it under the bunk in the corner and ran through the unlocked door, grabbing Eloise by the shoulders to keep her in front of him. Reaching the end of the hall, Dave flung her and himself to the right on the floor.

The explosion came as a dull, muffled thud that in a fragment of a second boomed into a shocking explosion that blew out the back wall of the jail and quaked the wall separating the cell from the office.

A cloud of grey smoke smelling of nitrates blew into the office, enveloping the crumpled figures on the floor.

Hardisty came running in and knelt over Eloise and Dave.

Other than being shocked by the suddenness of Dave's action and the subsequent explosion, Eloise was all right, but Dave was only half-conscious, and a trickle of blood came from his left ear.

The mob became a tame group of men who wished they were somewhere else. A few looked inside and saw Dave on the floor.

"Bomb! It was a bomb!"

"Somebody put it through the back window —"

"Who . . . ?"

"He must've set it off himself!" Gus Fallon roared unconvincingly.

"Not likely . . ."

The men dwindled away in silent pairs and threesomes, not talking much, just wanting to put some space between themselves and what was once an angry, mindless mob.

Leaving Eloise in Hardisty's care, Dave limped out into the street, saw the disillusioned mob drifting away, and then saw the bulk of the black-clad Gus Fallon farther on up in the middle of the street.

Wiping the dust and smoke from his eyes with his sleeve, he looked again to make sure, then stepped forward into the thin light.

Big as Fallon was, he was hard to see in the combination of moon- and reflected lamplight. The pallor of his face and hands was clear, as well as the glint of the brass star on his breast pocket, but little else.

"Fallon!" Dave's clear voice carried up the street, and froze the few hangers-on for a moment, and then they scattered for cover.

"Cromwell, I been lookin' for you!" Fallon yelled.

"You're finished here, Fallon."

Fallon was facing him, walking slowly forward, hands and face like white moths, the sheen of brass aglow.

"Like hell!" Fallon roared back.

Suddenly the two white moths swooped downward. Dave's right hand stabbed to the familiar butt of the forty-four and locked on, and the elbow lifted and raised the gun in one motion to aim at the gleam of brass.

In the near darkness two guns bloomed gouts of orange flame where the moths had been and Dave felt a burning pain in his side even as he squeezed the trigger.

The golden shine disappeared and the white moths swirled away, then dropped in the dust of the street.

Dave dropped to one knee to ease the pain, but it only grew worse.

Holstering the big gun and holding his side, he staggered back into the lighted jail, where Hardisty grabbed him.

"Lie down on the desk!"

"Yessir," Dave said, as if he'd been a naughty boy.

Eloise came to support his head in her arms as Hardisty tore at the bloody shirt, exposing his torso.

The raw gash across his side welled with blood.

"It'll clean itself out," Hardisty said. "Another inch and you'da had a digestion problem."

"Oh, Dave!" Eloise said anxiously. "I'm so sorry! Does it hurt bad?"

"Don't be sorry," Dave said, his face resting on her warm breast, his eyes looking up into hers, "I kind of like it this way."

# 12

*Die . . . !*

"That finishes it," Marshal Hardisty said, turning away from the heavy body of Roy Abbott flopped on the butcher block like a scraped hot carcass, the wires protruding from the fat neck.

"No, no, not quite," Dave said, walking away from the grisly scene.

Out in the dark street, he mounted Coalie and walked him over two blocks to the Abbott house. Lamplight came from the two front windows, and neighbors were already coming at this early morning hour to offer condolences and the strength of their company. They were closing ranks, bygones were bygones, and the survivors would stand together in their hour of need.

Mrs. Abbott sat in a rocking chair with her hands clasped loosely in her lap. Desolated, she had aged ten years in just the past twenty-four hours. Her grey hair had become silver and her features seemed to droop down without tension or foundation.

Her friends grouped around the rocking chair, touching her hair, caressing her shoulders gently, kissing her cheek, murmuring their support and common grief.

Dave found Eloise in the kitchen trying to make coffee and something to serve the guests, but the women took each small chore from her, grinding the coffee, boiling the water, adding wood to the fire, cutting up whatever cake they'd had or putting cookies on a serving dish, leaving her to stand by, watching numbly, her eyes dead tired.

"Take her outside, Dave," Ma Dove said. "Talk to her."

Without speaking, Dave took her arm and guided her out into the simple backyard with a vegetable garden in one corner and a hen coop in the other.

"I mean to get the jasper that did it," Dave said when they were alone.

"No, Dave," Eloise murmured, "I want no more blood shed. I never did."

"Eloise, that man killed a dozen people. Nobody can just walk free from that."

"It's over," she said. "There aren't any left. Please don't take any chances, Dave. I don't know . . ."

"You don't know what?"

"Maybe it's not ladylike, Dave, but I

want to say I don't know if I could bear losing you too."

From the dark prairie to the west came the long, mournful wail of a freight train loaded with cattle going east.

"Ma'am —" Dave took her hands and said unsteadily, his thoughts now radiant instead of gloomy black, his heart full of hope instead of sadness, "I'm comin' back, and we can talk some on what's ladylike and what isn't."

Suddenly she kissed him full on the lips, sending an electric shock clear to his heels, and with that she turned away, able to face the grim task ahead.

Dave mounted Coalie as he heard the freight's iron wheels screech on the rails and cars rattle and clash. It would load up with water and coal and soon be on its way to an eastern slaughterhouse.

He rode down First Street to River Road and turned right. Yonder was the railway trestle spanning the river, off to the east was Smoky Hill that rose above the river, crowded with new graves.

Turning left, he took the winding trail to the summit of the hill that overlooked the long valley where a shade of pink lighted the eastern horizon, sending the stars to bed.

Where the top flattened out to a level bench, Dave saw his man kneeling by a grave, a tall angular man without a hat. Dave stopped Coalie, letting the man say his prayer.

After a minute the tall man rose and turned to face Dave, who had dismounted and was walking forward, his hand brushing the butt of his six-gun.

"Hello, Dave," Tyson Tuck said. "I kind of thought you'd be here."

"You carryin' any baling wire with you?" Dave looked steadily up into the craggy face and deep-set eyes.

"All finished with wire, Dave. I hate the stuff."

"Why'd you use it then?"

"Tell you. If they'd shot him, I'da used lead. If they'd knifed him, I'da used steel — but they hung him, and they got equal treatment."

"Your brother?"

"We called him Babe because he was the youngest, but he was a man, and he left ma and us and his bride-to-be to mourn."

"And avenge him," Dave said slowly, watching the tall man closely.

"It's our way. Somebody comes against one Maclanahan, he comes against us all. I thank you for mailing his letter and doing your best for him."

"So you're not Tyson Tuck."

"No. Tuck Maclanahan from Kentucky is right. I couldn't say it before, or they'd all scattered."

"How did you manage?"

"The Mexican, Luis Javier. He's a good all-round man, and loyal."

"What about the saloon?"

"You know, back in Kentucky we say if you got somethin' you don't want, you trade it for a dog, then you drown the dog and you're rid of both of them," Tyson chuckled.

"So you plan on goin' back just the way you came?"

"Yes, unless you propose to stop me."

"I'm thinkin' on it. There's so many dead . . ."

"Including Babe," Tuck groaned. After a moment he regained his composure and his easygoing drawl. "I'm not armed, but even so, I don't think you can keep me from goin' home."

"I don't think I want to even try." Dave relaxed. "It's a long way."

The train hooted anxiously in the railroad yard, and they heard the clashing of iron car couplings as it started off.

"Like the traveler said to the Arkansas farmer, 'Is it a long way to town?' 'No,' the farmer says, 'it seems farther than it is, but you'll find it ain't.'" Tuck Maclanahan chuckled again and started down the trail.

Dave watched him go, his long legs stretching out and carrying him deceptively fast.

The train lost its speed at the rise of the bridge, and Dave saw the tall, gawky figure wait for the caboose to come by, grab a handrail, and swing up to the platform.

At the top of the bridge Tuck looked back and waved.

Dave lifted his hand and looked east over the new graves to watch the sun rise.

# About the Author

*Jack Curtis* was born at Lincoln Center, Kansas. At an early age he came to live in Fresno, California. He served in the U.S. Navy during the Second World War, with duty in the Pacific theater. He began writing short stories after the war for the magazine market. Sam Peckinpah, later a film director, had also come from Fresno, and he enlisted Curtis in writing teleplays and story adaptations for *Dick Powell's Zane Grey Theater.* Sometimes Curtis shared credit for these teleplays with Peckinpah; sometimes he did not. Other work in the television industry followed with Curtis writing episodes for *The Rifleman, Have Gun, Will Travel,* Sam Peckinpah's *The Westerner, Rawhide, The Outlaws, Wagon Train, The Big Valley, The Virginian* and *Gunsmoke.* Curtis also contributed teleplays to non-Western series like *Dr. Kildare, Ben Casey* and *Four Star Theater.* He lives on a ranch in Big Sur, California, with his wife, LaVon. In recent years Jack Curtis published numerous books of poetry, wrote *Christmas in*

*Calico* (1996) that was made into a television movie, and numerous Western novels, including *Pepper Tree Rider* (1994) and *No Mercy* (1995).